Everything I'll Never Tell HER

A Novel

Wieland Strasser

Please send all requests, questions, or feedback to
hello@8bcpublishing.com.
We are happy to hear from you.
www.facebook.com/8BCpublishing
www.instagram.com/8BCpublishing

ISBN 978-3-949152-10-8 (paperback)

For the eternal morning

~~~

SHE has broken up with me. Or has she? Let me quote Albert Einstein: "Some men spend a lifetime in an attempt to comprehend the complexities of women. Others preoccupy themselves with somewhat simpler tasks, such as understanding the theory of relativity."

I'm still lying in the green grass processing the phone call. "I don't know what I want—maybe I haven't experienced all of it yet. Anyway, it's all getting too constricting for me!" SHE said and hung up.

If we men are not to blame for a breakup, then we at once conduct research regarding the cause of it since it can't be our fault, at the very least. With HER, I spent the most beautiful days of my life. We talked, laughed, cuddled, and spent time in a meaningful way.

It was perfect.

I, the forty year old; SHE, the slightly younger one. I, the double divorcee; SHE, the one experienced in relationships. Both with a child from a previous relationship. The classic deterrents in a new relationship—such as "Eww, he already has a child!"—were done with, and so was the issue that there were already plans for many weekends. Both carrying understanding and flexibility to incidences concerning the children. SHE, the attractive one with waist-length, brunette hair; I, the slightly white graying one. Both similarly tall.

The call happened yesterday. After a sleepless night in which I explored every imaginable corner of my bed and considered the TV program at four a.m. not worth paying attention to, I am now lying in the fresh June grass on the banks of the Danube in my hometown of Linz. The earth is still damp. My toes recognized it immediately when I took off my shoes. It feels good to touch the cool moisture; I recognize now that I can still sense something. At least with my toes. My heart just feels pain. The Danube is passing gently close by and surely takes all my heartache with it from Central Europe to the Black Sea. Vast amounts of tears will eventually commune with the Atlantic Ocean after a long journey with those of others around the world and—"Oh, I don't care what anyone else's tears do!" I mutter to myself under my breath.

I am caught up in my Weltschmerz. The heart wants to burst, the belly wants to go to HER, and the mind tries to make me realize that the saying of all grannies and mothers will always remain valid: "There are plenty more pretty daughters that will match." I usually respond with, "Yes, mine is probably a Chinese rice farmer's wife!" By now, only I can laugh at this joke.

I just thought SHE was a match—a match for me.

Stop! A match does not quite hit it. *Ideal!* My Jill! The missing shoe to the entire pair! My absolute dream woman! I can only bestow superlatives on HER. However, in the next moment, I adopt the attitude that what happens in nature, society, and relationships is inevitably determined by fate.

The twist of fate is inescapable, and therefore my human volition is powerless. It is easy to influence it, but then again, only partially. It is like a book of many pages, wherein it already says in short sentences what will happen, but what precedes and follows, you can write yourself. Or, expressed poetically, fate is like the sky with many stars that everyone can arrange for themselves. They are there, but they can still be put in the right order. Only they were HER stars and not mine. My order would have been different.

At that moment, I notice two things. First, it's wet; the ground really is not yet comfortable to linger on. Second, I take refuge in fatalism. It helps me immensely in this moment in the decision to have some breakfast and to drive away the gloomy thoughts, which are immediately led ad absurdum upon the demand for one—no, TWO bottles of tequila. "As if I could survive two bottles of tequila," I mutter to my unwashed face.

The way to the favorite café is quickly identified. The "Cubus," located in the modern Ars Electronica Center Museum—called AEC for short— is hard to miss, especially at night with its bright flashing colors. During the day, it looks deliberate, like a stranded container ship that has drifted into Linz. The glass facade sparkles in the morning sun and calls out to me in a conspiratorial voice. Not to drink tequila, but to awaken my spirits with a coffee.

I guess it's a thousand steps. Just across the busy bridge, and I'll be there in a minute. No thoughts about the phone call—just pure concentration on every single step. "One, two, three, why do I like her so much? Six, seven, eight, nine, it was going perfectly until yesterday noon. Eleven, twelve—" Pause.

"Screw counting," I say in a low voice and hurry to the café quickly, running across the bridge so that it doesn't swallow me up. That mean, sneaky water calling out to me. *Jump! It's easy, no more heartache!* An imbecile thought, and then I remember "Ain't No Sunshine" by Withers and hum it for the rest of the steps. My mood is truly down the drain. *Why haven't I got this song on my iPhone?*

Something I'm going to fix as soon as possible. Weltschmerz would be so close to me then, cranked up loud. *Oh, isn't self-pity beautiful?*

I have arrived with a magnificent view overlooking the Danube, in the park that extends alongside it. It has an air of tranquility. In safety!

I may pursue my basic needs: food, drink, friends, love.

"Damn!" I shout, as if I were the only one here. Gina, my favorite waitress who has known me for a long time, looks at me sternly for a moment.

"There are other guests here," her look kills me. Oh, if only she knew what happened! Though, she is a woman—perhaps she can guess? The power that unites all Venusian women will have told her. Foolish thought. Anyway, from now on, I will watch her suspiciously to find out if she already knows in her mind what has happened. At that moment, I realize that I return to this magnificent glass building too often. It's my second living room, so to speak. I let my gaze drift. A woman with a dog is looking at me for a long time. *God, people are curious!*

Without inspiration, I order the next best breakfast on the menu and let my thoughts roam. I wonder whether I shouldn't call all my friends so that I can share the misfortune with them. Well, Michael already knows, even if he didn't really want to know. But what are best friends for, if not now? And for the first time, I have to smirk. Another thought is interfering with the grin. I want YOU back. I want a schmaltzy Hollywood ending and not one of the typical Austrian European films, which are probably closer to reality. I want feelings! I'm a contemporary man, so I want that too! But how?

How do I get this woman back? How can I convince HER that I am the one SHE needs, that I am the missing shoe! I must have a hit; I'll probably have only one try! If I screw it up, there will be no amicable breakup, but SHE will become a fury. One of such an ex-wife is more than enough for me; a second one in my hometown would be terrifying. By then, at the latest, I would have to find a new town, because Linz is not that big to warrant leading a carefree life. She could turn any corner at every instant.

The pen just darts across a quickly borrowed sheet of paper. Gina surely already worries about the well-being of the guests, because I'm muttering loudly, cursing, and laughing while collecting ideas. The egg—no, the entire breakfast sits untouched beside me in the meantime. Even the coffee has gone cold.

Never mind. Cold coffee is good against wrinkles and, after all, I am already forty!

I have created a masterpiece. In front of me is a multitude of ideas that only need to be validated and put into action to receive the prize instantly. HER!

Without thinking any further, I order flowers online from the homepage of a florist, thus checking off the first item on my list. In my mind, I bid my thanks to the gentlemen who invented smartphones. I thank God for the Internet, and at the same time I don't know whether he is pleased about all the sexual debauchery in the data jungle.

Red? Yellow? Multicolored? Roses? Spring bouquet? I'll go with something colorful because my mind is colorful right now. I am whipping out the credit card, entering the details, and failing. I fail at a mundane thing: I don't know HER address.

I mean, I already know where she lives. I know her last name, too. But I don't know the street. It was always at night and as a resident of Linz, I don't know my way around over there. What is this all about? Linz is divided into two parts by the Danube. Linz City in the south, Linz/Urfahr in the north. Those who live in the south rarely come to the north, and those who live in the north rarely come to the south, and if they do, they only pass through. Of course, this is an exaggeration, and any resident of Urfahr would rightly reprimand me for this foolish thought.

There are simply not enough bridges in the city that invite you to stroll over and explore the other part of the town. And yes, that includes me. Would Pöstlingberg be enough? About 2 km to the left? Or is it only one?

The first obstacle. No, I will certainly not drive to HER door and take a look. And if I disguise myself as a cyclist and happen to be cycling uphill? Do flowers even do the trick? How about a route planner?

It could go wrong, of course, because the messenger is in a bad mood, thereby screwing something up, thereby upsetting her, or perhaps the arrangement of the flowers is unappealing.

Time for a break. Time for my beauty coffee because it has already cooled down.

Why am I sitting here now? Looking out across the Danube and immersed in human sugar-sweet self-pity, I am mashing my brain and mashing my heart over and over again from the beginning.

"Hey, what's going on?" Gina asks.

Completely oblivious to the fact that she's suddenly sitting across the table during a brief break from serving me. I tell her in rough outline what happened and try to leave the impression that it's not so bad after all. I am a man and not a little boy anymore. Something like that doesn't hurt so much when you're grown up, I always thought. But no matter how old you are, heartbreak hurts. Gina listens to everything; she is my center of tranquility at that moment. Only when I'm done, she asks if I want to hear her opinion. *Of course, what can happen?* I think to myself and nod. Exactly what I didn't want to hear—and deep down, I know she's right.

"It just didn't work out, and somewhere there's someone who wants the same thing as you and that's exactly what *YOU* deserve too. You will see; in time, it will get better." What she says sounds logical, but I can't understand it right now, and I don't want to.

~~~

It all started on one of those days when you ignore the alarm clock several times, think to yourself that this is another ordinary working day in an ordinary life, and get up anyway. You spend hours in the world of work, which is satisfying from a professional point of view but often doesn't get you anywhere as a human being. Then, in the evening, you meet up with your friends who share the same fate and also want to escape into a mind-numbing TV program.

So we meet, the conspiratorial men's round of five, more or less experienced, men of different characters and appearances, having endless conversations that fortunately never become monotonous and drinking alcohol, or at least pretending to stomach it. At home, no one is bothered if we have drunk too much wine, beer, or something else that clouds our minds. We talk about anything we can think of. About trivial things, about banalities, and manage to make something meaningful out of the most unimportant stuff by adding ideas, sayings, and so on. It was at a classic guys' night out where I met HER.

Over the course of an evening, I may meet a lot of women. Sometimes, they get your full attention because they just look attractive. Other times, they don't attract your interest at all, even though they smell like sex, their pupils are large, but you are not interested at all in changing your dull-witted melancholy.

There are evenings that do not want to be bothered by flirtation. However, there are also situations where one longs for human attention, for a feeling of waking up in the morning and finding human warmth next to you. This time, we planned a wine night. We just wanted to be men. Talking stupidly, tastelessly about women, answering to no one, making crude male jokes about women. It started out as such. Built up to it and before we knew it, the whole place was our playground, and we were the stupid clowns in a crowd of unfamiliar, interchangeable faces. And SHE was not part of it all. Like a rock, SHE ignored us and yet SHE took part in our conversations. With HER beautiful, brunette hair, her height only slightly smaller than mine, and HER piercing green eyes, SHE fixed me. I was just too drunk to notice it right away and even more drunk when we briefly engaged in conversation. I can no longer remember the conversation, only that I suddenly felt comfortable in HER proximity; I was captivated by HER warmth. But I was torn away from HER. Loudly jeering, the whole party moved to another place. I was ripped away from HER so quickly that I—when I lost contact with HER eyes—no longer felt HER warmth but only the cold.

The next day, I was missing a few items that I thought were in the restaurant and when I entered it in the early afternoon, I saw HER again. To this day, I don't know what SHE was doing in the restaurant so early. I only know that that day, I fell in love with HER. At least, it warmed my heart. Over the course of four weeks, this conversation was followed by several more, often very short, exchanges until we agreed to meet for a coffee. Me, HER, and some years of our age difference—a circumstance which didn't seem to matter to me at that time, because nothing in life can be limited by age. Studying, working as a waitress, SHE gets herself and HER son through the week and still has time and the mood to conjure up a seductive smile on HER face. SHE appears to me eloquent and educated.

It was important to me to take it slowly. Not to destroy it with a hurried one-night stand. Not to push HER. I am in love, torn. I would like to guard HER like a treasure, which cannot be possible because nobody is "owned." The afternoon flies by and the next evening takes us over the rooftops of Linz. The event is called "exhilaration," wherein water installations as works of art sit atop interconnected inner city rooftops, open to visitors until late at night. A wall of fog forces us to find our way, holding hands with zero visibility. A touch that electrifies one. Water games are an invitation to linger for hours, entwined.

It was supposed to end after the tour up high, but we arranged to just snuggle due to the excessive amount of red wine we drank afterward. I opened the door, and we lapsed into a sex frenzy, the traces of which on my upper arms and back I will bear today and for the rest of my life. We kissed; we were all over each other. We forgot about time and space, we felt the sexual tension, we hurt each other, we reconciled, and we climaxed together several times. It was brilliant. Scars for life on the upper arm. For me, that night and morning could never have ended. I wanted to freeze time. I would become an inventor to preserve these beautiful moments. But I was in charge of my son, she had to fetch her son, and the little time with my son is just sacred to me. I had to leave HER.

Due to scheduling problems on both sides, there were only a few more nice evenings that did not end together due to various incidents. Then, there was a wonderful morning that passed so quickly that I thought that must be the kind of state for which the expressions "timeless" as well as "eternal" were invented. As if we had all the time in the world. Until I got this call.

Michael always says, "Such a short time—not much can have happened!" But for me, more has happened. I'm forty years old, have had two marriages, several long-term relationships, and numerous affairs. I know when a wonderful, precious person has slipped away from me. But as it is in human interaction, both have to want it. And SHE didn't want it. Is SHE sure, or did SHE think it through? Or was the sentence "I am afraid not to have experienced everything yet!" once casually said by HER taken more seriously than SHE meant it?

I have my list with which I can win HER back. I look at the writing and know, no matter what I do, it will not cause a positive reaction in HER. No flowers, no handwritten letter that I have already drafted in my mind, no social network will ever bring

HER back to me. I lost HER before I even got to know HER. All I will have left are the visible scars on my body.

"Another coffee?" Gina snaps me out of my reverie. By now, it is much later. I answer no, pay my bill, and earn a worried look from her. She looks as if she would like to ask me something, hug me, and squeeze me. I must look like shit. Tucked into bed at home, I torture myself into the night until I fall asleep, exhausted. The thought that maybe I was just a one-night stand to finish off HER previous relationship, to take revenge on the men, lulls me to sleep. The text from Michael, "Don't take it so badly, you'll be fine," I leave unanswered.

Yet it happened. In the last few days, I have seen HER three times. Short, fleeting encounters that always included HER child or my son. SHE even sent a text shortly after. "Was strange today. Without my son, I would of course react differently—just wanted to let you know, hope you're well. CU," it said.

So I wrote a letter. Seven pages full of energy and Weltschmerz. There was no other way; the letter had to be written. With sentences like: "I have never fought for a woman. If she wanted to go, I let her go. With you, it's different. You showed me in just a few hours what is possible in a relationship. You showed me in just one morning how and where to feel at home, to have arrived with someone."

And now I'm sitting here, in my night bar, my favorite place, and I face the problem that SHE, too, has chosen this place as her extended home. SHE has thus penetrated into my refuge, which I, in fact, have used to escape from HER, and SHE comes up to me, "Thank you for the letter. I was very pleased." A small pause follows, HER eyes fixing a gaze in the distance, looking for help.

"I know that this must have taken a lot out of you."

No, I'm sure it didn't—IT had to come out, I think to myself, instead saying in a way that was far too chilly, "So?"

SHE looks at me for a moment. "No, I—"

"Thanks, I don't want to know because I wouldn't understand," I interrupt HER and look past HER.

A sad glance hits me. I have the feeling that SHE still wants to tell me something at this moment. I remain seated for a few minutes after SHE stood up and returned to HER table. Then I leave the restaurant, join my friends, and start to get drunk. My friends do not know that I have just met HER. Nor should they, since I don't want to explain, I don't want to talk; I just want to drink. Drinking to numb all the thoughts so that they don't reach me anymore and I can stop thinking. I try to grab every little thing that comes up in conversation and turn it into something funny.

I feel like I'm seventeen because I raise my glass at every stupid remark and say things like "Down with it," "Chug-a-lug," and so on. Soon, the desired feeling sets in, and my thinking decelerates until I get into "standby mode." My body is present, but in my mind, everything is cloudy and I feel carefree.

~~~

"What the fuck?" the voice chimes from the phone. My head feels empty and dull. "What's wrong with you?" I'm lying in bed the morning after, still with no idea who's talking to me on the phone, and I feel sick to my stomach. I want to relieve myself, and the memory of the taste of vomit makes me drop the phone and disappear to the bathroom where I throw up.

"I hate this!" I yell into the foul-smelling toilet bowl in between bouts of relieving myself. Later, I stagger back to bed and check to see who that rude caller was. Sarah.

A call at noon—way too early after that night I can't remember.

Sarah—tall, blonde—is the failed experiment of a blind date from the internet. I met her on a dating site where I often met desperate women who were longing for at least a few hours of togetherness. Initially, I had contact with these kinds of women only. It was easy and convenient for me because I got what I wanted. But I also met women who considered this medium a way to meet other men than in the places where they went on weekends. And there were certainly a lot of lame ducks among them.

Anyway, I met Sarah, and I initially thought I could certainly drag this attractive woman into bed. Instead, I met a confident woman firmly rooted in her life, always looking forward. Shaking hands, we both knew at that moment it would not be enough for an intimate relationship, not even for an intimate touch. But over time, we found a companion, a confidant with whom we could share just about anything. Even if I scare her with some topics, she listens and delivers her comment on it, or I do when she tells me again about her lovers or her life experiences. I always have to smile when I think about her. Luckily, we live far away from each other; otherwise, we would just sit in cafés and philosophize about all the world and his wife. That would inevitably lead to my financial ruin once again. So, it usually stays within the realm of intense contact by e-mail; even talking on the phone often doesn't work. Either one of us is in a short-term relationship or so busy with work that we are not available.

"Why the hell did she call me?" I think to myself and call her back.

"Thrown up?" I hear her laugh through the phone. I still can't clearly assign her dialect to a region in Austria.

"Yes, there should be nothing left in my stomach now."

"I realize you probably have no idea what you have done today at three in the morning?"

I realize that my brain is not yet ready to carry out such complicated trains of thought and ask uncertainly, "No, what should I have done?"

"Go take a shower now, then check your status on Facebook, and then when you've sobered up, call me again. Ciao!"

That's my Sarah. Sometimes short and concise in her choice of words, while other times she can talk nineteen to the dozen but still finds time to breathe and thus leaves her counterpart the opportunity to interject a comment, while sheer brilliance comes out of her mouth. She is simply different from the other women I have met so far. Ok, except for Laura, another acquaintance. In one person, she is a combination of a friend, a listening ear, and someone to lean on. She even understands basic Martian, and I can trust her. I wonder what she would do as a lover. But then she would be too perfect.

I stare at the phone for far too long. My brain is still in hibernation mode; my limbs remain in a dormant position. "Showering would be a good idea," I mutter, suppressing the feeling to immediately look up what I've probably done on Facebook.

Anyone who has ever experienced intoxication knows the pleasant feeling when lukewarm water runs down the body and restores small parts of the spirits. This, however, is only temporary and ends abruptly when the stream of water runs dry. With the laptop in my hand, I drag myself back to bed, half wet. A hangover is simply better survived lying down.

Thirty-six new comments. *Not a good omen,* I think to myself and then check my Facebook status:

"Why the hell do women hate me? Why can't I find the one, and actually, I just wanted to fuck her!" Pause in my thoughts, then no pause—too many ideas rolling around and not allowing clear thinking.

"Damn," I curse. It doesn't do so well with all the other superficial status messages on my profile page. The number of comments does the rest. And you can see there are clearly two camps. Those who see it as misogynistic ("What happened to you, posting shit like this?") and those who are amused by it. *I'm glad these aren't my actual friends,* I think to myself, still drunken, dozing away. Unfortunately, SHE is also among my Facebook friends. I better not check if SHE is still one of them.

What feels like hours later, the phone brings me back to reality. "I only wear a towel. Otherwise, I cook naked," sounds cheerfully from the phone. Sarah is up to speed once again. "Now, tell me what happened yesterday? Or are you still too drunk?"

I take my time with the answer, thinking of her flashing eyes.

"I can only tell you eye to eye. I'll come to visit

you in the evening, and we'll discuss it over dinner, in a restaurant of your choice."

"Good, so at my place," and she hung up again. Happy about five additional hours of sleep, I turn over and fall asleep immediately.

~~~

Sarah doesn't live just around the corner but about 150 km away, and driving with a hangover is not necessarily fun. During the drive, I try to remember what happened, but only dark clouds of fog drift around in my head. The drive is unspectacular, and when I enter her apartment, I see the sparkle in her eyes. Sarah, tall, blonde—could there be a pattern?—always with a mischievous smile on her face, greets me in a towel. "Do you like it?" She kisses me briefly on the cheek and disappears seconds later in the living room.

Has she been wearing this towel for hours?

I follow her and begin wondering who her current boyfriend might be. A Spanish painter, a French general, a German millionaire, or a simple Austrian butcher? She's probably in a relationship with all of them at the moment, but of course I have no idea at all about her and her life aside from Facebook, texting, and phone calls.

Only rarely does she grant me a glimpse; usually, it's a thoughtless remark. It happens that I have known her for years, but it is absolutely unknown to me what kind of private life she leads. It has never been an issue between us. *Why don't I actually ask about it?* goes around in my head. A friendship between a man and a woman can work— you just have to define it. It should be no different than between friends of the same sex. We're friends, so why don't I just ask? Would she tell me, or does a "man" always want to sleep with a woman after all? The train of thought in my head is interrupted, and I look around.

The apartment is in orderly chaos, as usual. The couch looks as if breakfast and dinner had been eaten on it for the last three days. Next to it are her clothes from the last day. It is cozy and a warm, pleasant light fills the room. She always manages to create a homey atmosphere despite the mess and chaos.

I drop down with a loud sigh, feeling tired and burnt out. If relationships always end in deceit and deception, why not start that way? She probably has a boyfriend.

"Oh, I don't know," I suddenly start talking. Sarah sits there with her cushion tucked under her arms and looks at me with sympathetic eyes. "You know, every person is a unique narrative. So if we really want to get to know a person, we ask about their story. So, I probably wanted to know too much, too fast, too often.

"Was probably too close to her, and that's why she broke up with me. Oh, damn, I don't know and wouldn't understand her or you women anyway. Anyway, you lie in bed in the evening with open eyes and let the hours, days, go by in review to look for the reason. And the reason, after such a short time spent together, will probably be that SHE just wasn't interested in me." It just spills out of me. Sarah tends to be the kind of person who doesn't let others have their say. Now, however, she listens to my words with an alert mind. I watch her for a moment.

During the pause, she replies, "Listen, heartbreak hurts. That's just the way it is, and it happens to everyone at least once in a lifetime, or even more often. But it just wasn't meant to be. In life, things always turn out the way they are supposed to, even if you sometimes only realize the reason afterward.

"Maybe everyone has to experience real heartbreak once—to know what it is like to love and to be happy and satisfied at the same time. If you don't know the pain, you may not know how lucky you are to be loved. I once had a brief affair where I was really in love, and when it was over—on his part—I was miserable for almost a whole year. Every minute, I thought about him, and years later, there was an accidental encounter. At that moment, I knew it was exactly right the way it came to be. That man had no impact on me at all anymore, but I learned a lot for myself through him."

She nudges me on the shoulder and adds, "Everything will be alright; you will see."

"I had such a flow of energy with HER, though. Goosebumps when I touched her . . . it was just beautiful, to put it in unmanly terms. And SHE has deleted me on Facebook."

I think for a moment and then ask her, "I have never asked you how you imagine your ideal man, how things are in your love life, and what kind of relationship you are looking for. What defines quality for you?"

She looks around the room for a moment as if searching for a spot in the chaos. "A man who wears tight boxers, who is helpful and accommodating. He shouldn't smoke because I'm a non-smoker. Watches shows such as *Grey's Anatomy* with me without giving any comments and can cook, even if it's just spaghetti."

During the small pause, I want to reply something, but Sarah is in her element.

"A man who is just there, who puts his arm around me in the evening when I sleep until I need my own place to sleep. In front of whom I can think out loud and who sometimes brings a little something just because he wants to make me happy."

"Sarah."

"Who understands that you just want to be alone sometimes"—she found her spot in the room—"and who knows how I feel without me having to say anything, whose shoulder is there to lean on or even just to push away sometimes. And most of all," she takes a breath, "who sees me first in a crowded room!"

She has a sad expression on her face at this moment. Sarah, the strong one who always has an easy saying on her lips, at this moment shows a side of herself that I don't know.

After the conversation, I feel lighter, freer—I feel better.

Probably because other people feel the same way as I do, people who are searching and not finding. Surprised and amazed at what an accurate picture she has in her head, I am now convinced that she must have experienced more than I thought. We've known each other for years and talk about everything, but there are always moments that unearth new truths.

"Sounds pretty simple. Then what is it about you that always gets you into short relationships with men?"

Her facial expression changes again—she fixes me with a serious, no-nonsense look. "You know, I think it gets harder and harder the older you get. You just know what you want and what you don't; what you want to get involved with and what you don't. I don't need anyone to make me happy and content. I do well alone, but as a couple—when it works out—it's just nicer. And why lose time over something when you know in advance that it's nothing serious?"

Surprised by this statement, I get up and fetch us some wine. By now, I know where to find it and notice again that there is no hint of a man in this apartment, except for the slight mess. Afterward, we talk about how I met HER, how it fell out. Sarah doesn't let me peek behind her private facade now. When I fall asleep on her couch hours later, I feel her closeness. She is lying next to me and has fallen asleep, nestled deep into my shoulder. For the first time in days, I feel at ease. I stroke her head and fall asleep myself minutes later.

Sarah is different from all the other women I have met so far. She is brilliant in her own way. I wake up in the morning at seven a.m., and she is gone. No message, no text—nothing. With her, it's "Just go and close the door." My Facebook status: "Am confused, definitely don't understand Venusian, but am glad there are interpreters."

~~~

The letter I wrote to HER accomplished nothing. I have dismissed flowers. SHE avoids a conversation with a short shake of the head when we meet, and there are many such instances. Just yesterday, the two bookworms met at the bookstore. I walked into the bookstore; SHE walked out with a quick nod, a hand pointing to her son and a quick shake of her head. In the meantime, I see HER almost every other day, despite the effort I make to visit other places in Linz. For example, I have become a fan of the Donaupark. No pubs, only strollers, but on the way, there is the dangerous chance to see HER, so I have to cross the city. Hopelessly.

Now, I sit in the main square and enjoy the warmth of the sun, although, of course, I fled under a parasol. Even here, the waiter knows me; I go out too much, apparently. People in the main square are divided into those who sit in the café and look at the square and those who stroll there, observed by the others. There is usually a beautiful view that is only interrupted by sweaty biking tourists who pedal the last meters to a nearby hotel.

Some pause briefly at the Trinity Column that stands dominantly in the square. For many cyclists, it is a sign to have arrived in Linz and they take their first photos there.

I like this square where all of Linz meets. You realize that the city is too small to anonymously deal with one's heartbreak, because there are so many spots to meet HER. Like now, where SHE is sitting just ten meters away from me, drinking HER coffee. SHE is wearing a low-back dress; SHE loves to wear dresses. SHE looks beautiful in them. *Damn, I need to find a new city.*

Text to Michael: "Smack me in the face."

I have now moved on to the next option with the hidden agenda that I'm a pig anyway. Let's call it a "temporary solution." Michael thinks it's stupid; Sarah also doesn't think it's beneficial that I think I'm going to get relief for my soul through horny, meaningless sex.

"It won't make the pain go away; it will just move it backward in time. It's a distraction, but if it's good for you, go ahead. Have sex and let off steam," are her words. Despite everything, Sarah does not give me the impression that she is judging me.

Probably because she is a psychologist. But in the sight of HER low-back dress only a few meters in front of me, I am wildly determined. So, I want to fuck.

However, I am reluctant to do my rampant hustle and bustle in my hometown. I do not want the woman to suffer as I did with HER. So, off to the internet to look around in the singles' networks. How to do that? Just be smart, a bit cheeky when answering the profiles if you cannot score with looks, or you go through the trouble of switching to another city to find something with good luck. Much too exhausting. It's more comfortable from the couch or the café and is all done through the Internet.

I describe myself as "smart (makes sexy), masculine, honest, faithful, self-confident, not arrogant. My victim should correspond to the following description: positive charisma, satisfied with herself and balanced, of course, also reasonably presentable ;-) Age: about 30 years old"—and that's how the profile description could read. Women, I believe, have checklists—*long* lists that are checked before responding to a message. For example, we men are simply "ticked off" on the basis of trivialities: no appealing profession, no sense of humor, the eyes aren't attractive, the hands are too small, or the guy has a kid. Many pay attention only to the looks, and we certainly are not discussing now what 70 percent of all guys write in their profiles.

The easiest way is to respond to the checklist ironically. Write a funny comment point by point. While I never get letters myself, through some miracle, women reply to funny comments to their checklist. Whatever the case, I'm successful. One from Tyrol, one from Vienna named Natascha, and one . . . hmm . . . probably from Lower Austria fell into my trap. It is important to point out discreetly in the subsequent communication that one does not want to commit oneself in any case. The woman from Lower Austria recognizes my inferior motives and immediately removes me from her list of friends.

I cannot blame her. With my history, I no longer make a perfect son-in-law. At first glance, I appear to be a financial failure, incapable of having a relationship, and not shapeable. Well, on the subject of being unable to have a relationship, the first impression could also be right. Better yet, I also convey it.

The woman from Tyrol actually still clings to her ex-boyfriend and doesn't want to get involved in a sex adventure. If I were even meaner, I would say she would be something for later in about three weeks. The one from Vienna, however, is just on the hunt herself. *Emotionless, horny sex, here I come!* So, the Tyrolean was canceled and the energy invested on the Viennese. We write a few times, we talk on the phone and arrange a weekend when we both have time. There are clear rules. Have fun—no commitment. I am looking forward to it.

It's Friday night, and we've agreed that I'll come to her place around eight p.m. and I am responsible for the wine. She prepares a little something for dinner in return. She gave me her name, which is on the door, so it's no fake, no mirage—of which there are many on the net.

I find it immediately and ring the bell. A bit excited, I wait until I am let in.

Hopefully she looks at least somewhat like the picture she sent. *Yes, quite nice,* I think while she is opening the door for me. Black curly hair, green eyes, a feminine figure—exactly what I want. An erotic tingling is in the air. She invites me in and I follow her. The apartment is big—bigger than I thought. I don't look around closely because I'm not that interested; she has my full attention. She and every single part of her body that I will try to stimulate.

We sit down in the living room, cool but elegantly furnished. She works in the advertising industry; she is likely successful and earns a good living. She has style. Candlelight illuminates the room, and there is a plate of antipasti on the table. *The Bardolino I brought with me goes perfectly with it*, I think and smile. We eat a few bites, make small talk about the weather, the job. Magical glances are exchanged. The next moment, I just get carried away and throw myself all over her.

From one end of the couch, I move slowly toward her but fast enough to catch her off guard, grabbing her side with one hand and her head with the other. I kiss her—very cautiously at first and not too clumsily. A game of lips begins; she knows the game. It's good, I think, just brilliant, and when our tongues also make their appearance following our lip play, it becomes more and more passionate. The mood changes—no longer restrained, but demanding! Meanwhile, I lie on top of her and our pelvises search for and find each other. Too much fabric, too much on—take it off, *right now*. I want SEX. My fingers feel more and more, and I want everything. Simply everything.

I opened her blouse, or was it her? What I feel during a fierce kiss is blossoming, becoming hard. I start to play with it. I stroke, I scratch, I grab. A bite to my lip—not hurtful, but still very dangerous, warning with a mixture of palpable lust. In response, I turn her around, and she seems to know what I mean. She lets me turn her over and kneels in front of me. Too much fabric still, so I push up her skirt, pull her closer to me, and tug at my pants.

Damn—it's always in these moments I struggle to undo the buttons. Only seconds later, I am so caught up in the situation that I forget everything, press her against me, and slide into her to overcome the pressure. I take possession of the kneeling woman in front of me. It is violent, hard, exciting, and great at the same time. She is a stranger, does not know me, and lets everything happen to her.

It gets faster, harder, and I realize that we are both close to the end. Some thrusts, harder and harder, and yes, yes, yes . . . *Wow!* I think. We are both completely knocked out and fall asleep next to each other. The entire weekend, we have sex in every room, in every possible position. We understand each other without talking much and say goodbye on Sunday as if this had been a typical weekend. Kisses left and right, and we don't discuss if there will be a reunion because we feel that this was a once-in-a-lifetime opportunity. Text from Sarah: "You are a gigolo, a pig ;-) but enjoy it. I don't know you any differently."

Damn, I'm an ass. I get off the train in Linz, walk through one of the most beautiful station halls in Austria, and see HER standing at the ticket counter. Never in my life have I ducked away so quickly and looked for a way out. I have a guilty conscience. Such a guilty conscience. I feel guilty towards HER because I have cheated on HER. *Cheated?! Why the hell would I have cheated on HER?* I continue on my way home, shaking my head. Roaming home along the country road, I feel restless again.

When I get home, there are two new friend requests on Facebook. Request number one is Amy, a flirt from eight months ago who then decided to go back to her ex-boyfriend after too many texts exchanged between her and I in one day.

Why do all women go back to their ex? Am I that bad? Do women realize after meeting me that things can only improve after me, that there is nothing better to come after me? That the ex was a better choice that way? That might be a new line of business for me. "You want your ex-girlfriend back? Then let me go out with her. 100 percent satisfaction guarantee! You want proof? Look at my ex-wives and some of my affairs; they all went back to the boyfriend they had before!"

Number two is HER. Damn. After weeks of pain, alcohol, ignoring, and brief, fleeting encounters, SHE appears here. My first thought is to cancel my Facebook account and finally escape this social network. The second, whether there are any treacherous status messages of my suffering left online. Third, I immediately shut the laptop and go to bed just before ten.

Why the hell did she delete me and then add me again?

I wonder what Sarah would say to that. I text: "That's when I need you, and you're probably sleeping well, I hope."

No reply.

Why do women always have to go to bed so soon? Do they really need the beauty sleep so badly, or do they not want to conceal the traces of the night from their face the next day in a tedious and time-wasting way? I think it's a pity because the face is actually the reflection of life, and not a deceptive, rigid crust a few millimeters thick.

I have not slept, of course. I thought about turning on the computer a hundred times. Does SHE want anything?

Is there a chance?

Damn, do women see me as a father figure? Is it enough just to be good friends?

At five o'clock in the morning, I accept both requests and go for a run. It's raining in August. It's wet, it's cold, but I don't care.

When I come back, a text from Sarah greeted me: "Morning . . . was already asleep . . . sorry I wasn't there . . . did you need anything?"

The text arrived at half past six when I was running. The start of the working day for my friend Sarah. I would hate to have to go to work so early. I'd rather torture myself sleeplessly through the night and go running early. Stupid!

During the day, there is insignificant superficial communication with HER via texts.

HER: hey, pretty good, Paul was sick last week, now I spent a week in bed (at least I finally read the book for the bachelor thesis :)), otherwise always the same. how are you? move done?

ME: oh, you poor thing! but at least you didn't miss any nice weather!

HER: it was fine, anyway, it was super cozy, I wasn't sick, only Paul . . . So I was just a backup.

ME: I'm going on vacation with Benjamin in the next few weeks.

HER: super that finally everything worked out with the vacation with Ben. I'm going to Italy next week with 6 girlfriends for 4 days, will be super fun for sure—I'm almost a bit scared of it . . . somehow you could expect anything there—a bit like hangover maybe :)

ME: Yes, the hangover will certainly be terrible . . . incl. vacation flirts!! hopefully you'll see it while still sober.

It doesn't get any more superficial than that. At least that's what David, Michael, and Frank think while we're working out on the climbing wall. Michael says, "You should stop seeing several women at the same time."

"What do you mean?" I ask.

"HER, Amy, Sarah, Natasha—too many women in your life that you chase after. It's like an addiction with you!"

"No," I reply, "I am not with Sarah! I would never be, but otherwise, maybe you're right. I should stay away from women, especially from HER. And I should tell you guys less!"

"Then delete HER," my best friend retorts and pulls the rope so tight that Frank briefly yelps five meters above us.

"Stop talking about his love life! I don't want to fall off!"

When I get home in the evening, there's a message in the mailbox: "Do you have time for a meeting next Sunday? Swimming in the lake? In Attersee? Amy"

I look at the message for a second. At first, I thought it was from Sarah, then from HER, but it is from Amy, who does, in fact, have a boyfriend, or at least she thinks she is in a relationship with him. I answer positively and don't expect anything from this Sunday.

I see HER Facebook entry, "Looking forward to vacation soon!" and Amy's text, "looking forward to Sunday with you at the Attersee."

~~~

A storm is blowing. On my Facebook profile, it says, "It's stormy here at the Attersee, but I'm sitting here enjoying the atmosphere." I love this ambiguity. The truth is, we kissed. After Amy told me that she would keep trying with her boyfriend—because you should stand by your man even in bad times, even if he is seeing other women—we felt each other most intensely in the worst of the storm. For hours, we lay on the jetty while the weather around us drove all the people into the houses.

Do you understand women? It was good, and yet I am confused, kissing a woman who is beautiful, who is ten years younger and who, according to her, is in a relationship. I told Sarah, of course, and she responded with an e-mail:

i can't answer the question of what she intends by this. from my own experience, i know that i am different from everyone else . . . no one could understand me when my EX broke up with me and i waited months for him to come back . . . am maybe not the best person to talk to about this.

hmmmm, what could it be . . .

either she wants to take revenge on her boyfriend, get back at him, give him a similar feeling . . .

or she forgives him for the fling . . .

or maybe she is still too caught up in the old pattern. she can't separate from him yet . . .

or she just doesn't want to be alone, so she goes back to him and looks for a new one without being disturbed . . .

i often ask myself the same question with men. i've had a few guys lately who actually have a relationship. there has been the odd conversation that their relationship is not so good. that their relationship is not going so well and they can imagine a relationship with me. my question was always what makes me different from the current one. why shouldn't it be the same with me and having another one at the same time? well, with this question the dream was usually over . . .

apart from that, cheating doesn't necessarily count as a virtue for me. what everyone does while being single is one thing. but relationship is something else. and if she thinks that's ok, well . . . no idea . . . maybe i am just a burnt child . . . but i still think that there are two kinds of cheating . . . sex-and-that-was-it or maybe-not-yet-kissed-but-with-your-heart-at-it . . . whereby the second is clearly worse. when feelings are involved, it can become dangerous.

I like my Sarah. She helps where she can, and at the moment, she really helps me. As I fall asleep, a text from her reaches me while I'm still drowsy: "You still owe me a dinner! I expect you to pay me back as soon as possible."

I answer, "Do I have to cook naked?" and receive "Maybe, good night," back.

Right after that, there's another text from Amy: "lying in the bathtub with a smile on my face." I am fast awake at once. Too many women in my head. In my mind's eye, I see another sleepless night ahead of me and decide to wander through the city. After a short walk, I stop at the Taubenmarkt square. It is midnight, and the fountain in the center of the square is quietly splashing away. Sunday in Linz is always deserted, extinct on this day and at this hour. Sitting down, I notice that, apart from me, only one couple is lingering in this square. Judging by their posture, newly in love, they want to touch, kiss, and feel each other.

If only they knew what will happen to them after the days of rose-tinted glasses have passed and everyday life has caught up with the relationship. It's nice to watch when others are literally struck by lightning. And it hurts me. From a distance, I glance at the beautiful couple. He looks up, and his gaze passes over me. On his forearm is a tattoo that resembles a snake.

She looks after him in my direction. SHE.

It is HER.

While I have just given HER a scare, I want to drown myself in the fountain standing next to me. No hello; I simply freeze as SHE urges him to get up and move on. SHE is wearing a beautiful red dress that ends over the knee and looks stunning in it. I think of Michael's words and my current relationship with women and think about giving in to the urge to becoming a diving instructor on a desert island. But what keeps me in Linz? Benjamin, my son. A solid rock in the flood that is about to break over me, leaving a huddled man alone in a deserted place.

My Facebook entry: "Tried to drown myself in the fountain at the Taubenmarkt today." Eighteen people like this entry; one thinks that this is pollution. Therefore, I have one FB friend less: HER.

~~~

"I don't like you," I start talking to Sarah when I fulfill my promise to cook for her. "'I don't like you,' my son said to the only girlfriend I ever introduced to him after the divorce."

There is a pan on the stove in which vegetables are being briefly sautéed. From next to that pan drifts the aroma of spicy fried scampi. I look for oil in Sarah's kitchen, who is sitting at her kitchen table watching me cook for her.

"I don't think any man has ever cooked for me in this kitchen before!"

"Sarah, I'm beginning to think no man has ever cooked for you; they're more likely to take you out."

I'm getting hungry as I gather all the ingredients.

"One of my dilemmas is I need to find a woman who gets along with my son. He can just be very mean and straightforward at his age. Luckily, that's puberty, but with the girlfriend at that time, it made such an impact that she managed not to get in touch after just five days."

"I'm beginning to think it's you," Sarah says as her eyes flash at me.

"Sure, I'm misogynistic, stubborn as a mule, and I didn't do the charming thing. And of course, at my age, I have certain expectations that have to be fulfilled, or habits that I won't give up. Scampi?" I push a bite between her teeth to take the wind out of her sails right away.

"Did you actually cry terribly five days ago?" she sneers at me.

"The fountain certainly needed new fresh water afterward, and I was amazed at how strongly it overwhelmed me, but the funny thing is that so far, I haven't spotted any traces of HER new husband on Facebook." I notice Sarah's brief but fierce exasperated shake of the head, drain the water from the pasta, fold the pasta into the vegetables, and start to arrange everything on the plates.

"Looks delicious! I'm thrilled that you can recreate recipes from a cookbook." There it is again—

her mischievous grin. "Wine is already open and sitting in the living room."

"Which, by the way, is kind of tidy today! No tons of books and traces of work to be found; I'll just positively note here. Not that it would ever look better at my place." She pats me on the upper arm, grabs the plates, and disappears through the door.

"I think you women want to be unhappy!" I shout after her. "You'd much rather bitch about your partner or share your sorrow with your girlfriends, because it's much easier to be miserable than happy!"

Sarah somehow doesn't listen to me at all, but instead leisurely eats her pasta with vegetables and seafood. "You know, I would have liked to call you now and then so that you could come to my place to sleep with me, but you must live in Linz and arrange your life around there."

At this point, my chin has certainly dropped to the table.

"It would never work, a relationship with both of us! I wouldn't want it to, either, because if you were my boyfriend, I'd have to kill you, and the pasta with this balsamic sauce tastes excellent!"

"Thank you," I murmur, wanting to say something in reply but deciding instead to switch to more conventional, harmless topics and just continue eating.

The meal was so opulent that I just barely make it to her couch and lie down comfortably. Sarah sits at the other end of the couch. "Maybe you want too much? You want an attractive woman who will oppose you, who will support you, who will put up with your nonsense, and it's the latter that can drive a woman crazy. Do you have any idea how a woman will take it if you go climbing without telling her beforehand? You can be sensitive, and the next moment, like a Railjet thundering over regardless of the consequences, and now let's drop the subject! Maybe SHE also just wasn't interested in you anymore and simply chose the wrong words."

When something sinks in, it sinks in—like a punch in the gut. While I'm probably still looking at Sarah in bewilderment, she lies down next to me and, unusually for her, switches on the TV. *Am I really such an ass?* I think to myself, while I feel her by my side, *and why the hell did she want to have sex with me? I thought I was just a gigolo in her eyes anyway, who doesn't want to decide where he ends up and then eventually overlooks everything.*

I don't know what's going on, but suddenly I feel a second heart beating wildly next to me. The scent of "light blue" is in the air and clearly identifies her. Her skin touches mine, and when I meet her gaze and sink into it for a moment, I hesitate. I feel warmth and trust that I have never known before. I hesitate and do it for too long because she turns her head away and takes the television as a new fixed point in her life. She accepts the fact that I'm confused; perhaps she enjoys it.

As I lean back, I cross my arms behind my head and try to think. To analyze something, to switch on the logical mind and notice that I don't want to think at all but just let myself drift right now. I straighten up, pull her to me, and taste her lips. There's a hesitant hand on my belly that remains hesitant and touches me for the next minutes, hours, while I taste and feel her; I feel us and sink.

"I'm going to bed. You sleep here on the couch; you're panting too loud for me!" Standing naked in front of me, I recognize the dim outline of the woman I was exploring just minutes before. Her tone is clear, pure—no more excitement, no more hesitant touching. The distance is palpable again.

"Shall I bring you breakfast in bed?" No reaction; I can't even see if she's grinning, but she turns and disappears only to return moments later, press a fleeting kiss to my nose, and vanish. "Miss, I'm such a light sleeper," I mumble as I stare at the ceiling and start to overthink, tormenting myself with the thoughts. Or rather, I want to, but at last, for the first time in a long time, I don't manage it and am suddenly overcome by sleep.

Benjamin is an early riser. Whenever he's with me, it's possible that I'm woken up at six a.m. and told to be ready for nonsense. The problem I've had since then is this: Whenever someone is close to me, I'm awake around half past six. So at the moment, I'm lying on the couch and I don't hear anything. Not a sound from her bedroom. Although I know she is next door, there is no indication that she is there, that she is awake or, most importantly, what she is thinking. "Stop thinking," I hear her say in my mind. So, I get up, enter the bedroom, look her in the eye, and lie down next to her. Feel her. She crawls on top of me, puts her finger on my mouth, and lies on top of me.

Four hours later, I leave her apartment. For the first time in our long relationship, she kisses me on the mouth as I leave her apartment. When I turn around and look at her again questioningly, she says, "Don't think so much! You trouble your head more than I. I would like to watch right now what's going on in your mental movie projector!"

~~~

Amy's text: "I'd still like to see you again, even though I'm flying to the USA with him!" *Do you understand women?*

"You have done WHAT?" Michael says, choking on his beer. He is so loud that even SHE overhears it. Some time ago, I decided that I would continue to visit my favorite pub and not avoid it just because SHE is regularly found here in the evening.

All the old movie posters on the walls create a comforting, familiar environment. Outside in the summer and sitting in the basement in the winter. Yes, in the basement! But surrounded by this homey atmosphere, which you probably don't recognize as such in daylight, it's homey.

SHE brushes us with her gaze, because SHE— *oh, miracle*—happens to be right here. I just remembered that SHE didn't greet me with kisses today and that I forgot my apartment key at Sarah's place.

"Please don't confirm to me now that you're going completely crazy and dragging everything into bed that could wear a skirt! So you made out with Amy too, and then Sarah?" Michael's expression is serious. And this from the man who usually wears his life on his sleeve and can be read like a book.

"It just happened. She just told me to stop thinking, and then I just didn't think."

Michael speaks so loudly that even the twenty-four-year-old neighbors at the next table have noticed that it is about the common issue between men. While he still looks at me, twinkling, I notice that I absolutely didn't care if I got a little kiss from HER today. It's kind of gone, the self-pity. Sarah is simply the best. "I'm a pig!" I say to Michael, and at that moment I don't mean it as a reaction to

36

his statement towards me but as I notice the shock that I still feel something towards HER—but I remain emotionless. The armor should remain undamaged; I simply do not want to feel anything, and I console myself with the fact that Sarah seems just as cold as I am. After all, we have defined that it will never be enough for a relationship.

"Is it possible that I seem dysfunctional in a relationship?" Such sentences can really upset Michael and mess up his facial features. While he is talking to me, I discover HER boyfriend, who is just saying goodbye to HER with a kiss. *SHE has never done that with me,* occurs to me at that moment.

"Listen. You sacrifice yourself for friends. Always have time for others, even in your ups and downs. My point is, you're not cold, but you hurt; you want to hurt, and you do. Perhaps you also emanate this or convey this to your female counterpart—that you do not want to commit yourself but only seek temporary pleasure in order to then retreat into your shell. You have just come out of a deep emotional crisis that lasted for years and a financial disaster. Only months ago, you spent the night in an empty room surrounded by—I don't even *want* to know about everything that lived there.

"Anyway, you have passed through a deep valley, pulled yourself out of it by your own hair, and are now climbing your mountain again. You should probably wait until you have climbed the mountain and have a clear view of all around you again. And above all, keep your hands off women who are after providers. Yes, I know, that's unfortunately more than half of all women. By the way, David is single again."

"Really?" Gratefully, I grasp at straws to escape the scolding. "What happened?"

"Well, as it happens lately, she threw in the towel when the bad times started, and David had to take more care of his kids. He hid it well from you because he didn't want to burden you with it on your 'I-pity-myself-and-move-through-the-world' trip. Well, at least you gave up feeling sorry for yourself."

I think that's where my friend is wrong.

"Now tell me, what attracts you to HER, Amy, and Sarah?" Michael directs the conversation back to me. It was so nice to be able to change the subject and to know what happened to David. But I know Michael—better surrender to fate once he has stuck in a topic.

I take my time with the answer and look for HER in the busy room. See how SHE banters with a standard smile on her face with the acquaintances at her side. Thinking of HER soft hands that suddenly dug deep into my flesh.

Thinking of Amy's fingers holding me tightly, even though her head was running away, and Sarah's fingers touching me carefully as if I were an unfamiliar surface her fingers were touching for the first time.

I first try a joke. "My dream now, if you ask me like that, would be to have them all waiting for me in bed at the same time."

If the look had already been unique before, Michael's look now says that he finally considers me crazy. I surrender to my fate. "Joke! Each for herself has something unique. SHE is simply admirable for what she has been doing for years. SHE is well-read, and I can talk to HER about whatever I want. Plus, there was this morning that was just fantastic in my emotional desert. Imagine that in the desert, there is suddenly a lake the size of Lake Attersee. No wonder that then the green sprouts in such a way that nature would blossom. SHE is unique. I don't even want to talk about the sex; I had bruises all over for a week.

"Amy is simply beautiful. A top-notch woman. Please excuse this perhaps not-gender-compliant expression, but she is a blast. A woman who has an impact. I know from previous conversations that I can talk to her, and I love spending time next to her. Plus, she knows where to grab. There's just something about those blue eyes. And with Sarah," here I pause briefly and struggle for my words, "everything is familiar. The talking, the understanding, her body. Plus, she's a fantastic kisser." Michael looks more and more suspicious.

"Oh, I don't know. I haven't asked for this, what's happened in the last few weeks. It's just happened. I just have to be careful not to hurt myself again because then I'll screw something up! In my hormone-driven world."

"Let's cold-shoulder the girls," he is trying to talk to my conscience.

"Michael, I can't do that, and neither can you. I can only tell you that I felt at ease with all three of them. Very much at ease. But SHE made up some excuse that I still can't come to terms with, and besides, she's approaching us right now! Two more shandies, please!" I nod to the waitress.

She confirms it with a short nod.

I wonder what SHE was thinking the other day at the Taubenmarkt square? When I saw HER with HER new lover. I think to myself and continue to speak, letting my eyes wander restlessly over the crowd of people in the pub.

"SHE had it in her own hands and screwed it up, for whatever reason; I still don't understand. I would feel better with an explanation such as: 'It was just for a straw fire. It was only enough for a flash in the pan.' Amy, on the other hand, is so determined to be financially secure. Probably because of what she has experienced, she would rather satisfy her head than follow her heart. And of course, because of this statement of hers, I would have wanted to have her as a friend, anyway, with a certain uneasiness. And with Sarah . . ." I have to pause again and struggle for words.

"With Sarah . . . it would probably be different if we lived closer together. But this way, it would just end in a huge pain.

"Because I know myself.

"After months of going back and forth, I would then go out with a nice blonde, for example, and being the pig I am at the moment, I'm sure I'll flirt with her and hurt her and myself, which she doesn't deserve. And that's all because I want to stay here in Linz, for the reasons you know. On the other hand, she is a fascinating woman with whom a man can say what he has to say without being misunderstood, or at least he believes so. I also don't understand how a man could ever let her go. Ok, now, of course, you can say that I just shouldn't let her go. But I'm not supposed to 'capture' her at all. Oh hell, I don't know either!"

I break off, lean back, and look at my best friend. I think that Benjamin has it best at the moment, being a teenager who doesn't have to deal with complicated emotional entanglements yet.

"You should go ahead and then come back sometime when you've found yourself."

"Thanks, Michael, but you also know that I've only been doing better financially for a few months now, and I'm just happy to have found a cheap apartment for once!"

"Your beer! Nicole asked me to bring it to

you." I startle, look at HER, and suddenly have the feeling that SHE has been standing there for a few seconds longer and has picked up fragments. In any case, SHE looks at me several times in the next few minutes.

"Let's leave it for today. Rather, tell me what is going on with David; I don't want to deal with it now! Even if it haunts me tomorrow, Saturday, when I'm alone with myself! I have probably strayed from my path! Period!" Michael tries again to push forward with me, but I insist on the end of my narration and in return learn that the father of two, recently divorced, was left by his girlfriend when the quarrel with his ex-wife approached a new climax.

"It's a pity, because if that had passed, they would have known if they could encounter other storms with it." David, of course, is not doing so well. The only friend among all of us who can get all emotionally involved with a person. But it's reassuring to learn that we can provide a cushion for him and deliver what's best in a situation like this: listening!

At some point we pay, and in the process I have to walk past HER. SHE does still not hug me. On the way home, Michael drags me to another pub for a final beer. Loud Cuban music welcomes us. People are crowded together. We toast and see HER boyfriend just as he tries to teach another woman tongue acrobatics. Immediately, I snatch my iPhone, take a picture, then grab the beer and take a big gulp in a few fluid movements, as if I had practiced them many times. Michael notices nothing of it.

Pig! I think to myself as he tries again to remove her plaque with his tongue, and yet I am probably no better with Sarah or Amy or HER, although I am not with anyone. I am confused and notice that I would probably have to think about the term "relationship" more carefully. Should, want, or actually rather not?

Vibrations in the pocket with a message: "Hope you're having a good time with Michael! Sarah"

I was being mean. Certainly, it was exaggerated, but I went looking for a free ad space the next day that I was sure SHE would see on her way into town. This in itself was not difficult because there is only one main road leading from Pöstlingberg to the city. There, I had a poster put up showing HER friend during his tongue training session with another girl. A billboard. The fun was worth it to me. If you do publicly cuddle with young love, you must also take the consequences into account. I have not told Sarah this time yet. David found it amusing in his heartache. Michael, on the other hand, has given up on me being rational. I also don't know if SHE noticed; there is still no hint of him on Facebook, either of their relationship or hopefully its end. But when I look at her old posts, there's none about me either. It's like she's hiding HER relationships and not putting them out into the world. Unlike me, who wears his heart on his sleeve.

Damn it, I'm stalking HER. I'm an idiot.

Amy has no idea about all this while she is drinking a coffee with me with a view over the Danube. I don't want to let her in on it, either; I'd rather let her tell me about her perfect trip to the USA, emptying Victoria Secret's stores and enjoying romantic dinners, while my hand is still on her thigh and my lips are still guessing the taste of her lipstick.

She fantasizes about a life together with him at a lake while stroking through my hair, and for the grandiose ending, she throws the following at me so that I will continue to not understand women: "You know, with you, I can imagine a family, having children. But I stay with him because he offers me financial security. You're wonderful, but you're—how can I tell you now—you're certainly a perfect father, but I'm afraid of the child that's hidden very deep inside you. It is too erratic, and you have too little ambition in your job. I think I would have to kick your butt too many times because of it. And I'm especially put off by your financial fiasco after the divorce. I apologize for that, but in my life history, there have often been financial inconsistencies, and it is very important to me to be on the safe side here. You're wonderful; I can relate to you, you know where to grab, and you kiss better than he does. But I've set my priority. I hope you understand that."

Two deep blue eyes are gazing at me, appearing watery. I'm not the only one carrying my burden. Other people carry a heavy one, too, like our very own David. Some seek the easy way; others, the bumpier one. Others put their personal needs on the back burner and a few, like me, just drift along, unable to figure out anything.

One knows only at the very end which way would have been the right one, I think to myself while I let her talk. It is probably the last time I will see her. What a pity! Although she seems fixated on material things, I like her because she is honest, and I worry that she will fall into despair when she realizes that she is lying to herself. "Thank you for your honesty," I interrupt Amy during a short pause and grab her hand more firmly.

Yes, honesty or being honest with oneself is difficult, and there are many ways to persuade yourself to believe things until you actually do believe them. I also do that and I am a world champion in it, but I notice this "misbehavior" more in others. I don't want to see it in me and that's why I rarely recognize it.

Also, with my ex-wives, I knew before that something was wrong. I often told myself that it was okay if we didn't have sex anymore because we had been married for so long, but deep inside, I felt that it wasn't right. Not just with my divorces, but with other relationships, too. It had already ended, but as long as I didn't admit it to myself, my world was still a whole one. And that "whole" world is better than the one it's disintegrating into. It crumbles chunk by chunk until there is a pile of rubble and ashes. It takes a lot of work to rebuild this, and gradually you think you're going to break.

"It's not tragic, either. I expected it. Because you made it clear earlier, too." I pause briefly, wanting to let the following sink in.

"If you ever need help, tell me, call me—I'll come at any hour," I say it, and mean it, hugging her and earning a look from Gina that asks me, "How many more women do you want to come here with?" I realize that I really do come to my front living room for breakfast too often. Then again, the view overlooking the Danube is just so brilliant here in the Cubus.

When we pay, I still see Amy's moist eyes and bid her farewell with a kiss on the cheek. And a hug that lasts just too long to remain simply good friends.

I stand alone on the Nibelungen Bridge, which spans the Danube. The stream passes by leisurely, as late summer has set in. A single ferryboat is steaming against the current upstream towards Rotterdam, presumably. *That's interesting*, I think to myself. *Nothing is happening on the Danube, and on the Rhine, there's almost a traffic jam.*

Yet a woman is strolling across the bridge with her golden retriever, focusing on the ship while her dog is panting behind her. Like probably all the men she knows. Mean thought—I don't even know her. Though, she is attractive.

I don't want to go home yet. Therefore, I choose a deliberate detour home through the winding, narrow streets of Old Urfahr. The streets—or, rather, alleys, which for a moment remind me of a cramped Rome—are overgrown with old vines or ivy and become lighter towards the stream, inviting me to linger.

A call from my lawyer interrupts my thoughts: "The billboard company called because someone wants to know who ordered this billboard. In addition, there is the offense of property damage."

"Was my name passed on by you?"

"No. Only if there is a complaint from the person in question will I probably have to give you away."

"Good, let me know when you're going to turn me in to the justice system." I still don't care that I caused the trouble with the billboard. It's not my problem anymore, but no idiot who canoodles with strangers is worth being a more intimate part of HER life.

The route to the billboard is quickly found, as it is not far from my current location. "SWINE" is written there, in large letters, the "W" being illegible, as the wall has probably made acquaintance with a sledgehammer or some other hard, heavy object. His face is no longer recognizable. The poster was hit with great anger or force. Pieces of wood are still scattered on the street. I feel a lot—just no satisfaction. But I am not ashamed of it and would do it again immediately.

My legs do find their way home now. This day somehow didn't go as perfectly as I thought it would. Actually, it didn't go that way at all, but it's one of those days you remember years later. It's not an ordinary day that can be replaced at will.

Post on Facebook: "The truth lies in the demands you make on yourself, which you don't live up to. And the fear to adapt or the lack of courage to jump into the deep end. And now that I've come out of the latter, I'm going to bed! Bon appetit."

~~~

At the main square, I see HER. Her friends are with HER. They are sitting near the plague memorial and have HER hugged against them; SHE is crying. I stop and look at HER from a not-so-safe distance. HER gaze is silent as SHE stares blankly into my face for too long. Tears run down HER cheek. One of HER friends looks at me in surprise because SHE doesn't know me. I nod to HER; SHE does not nod back. Then I turn around and don't look back as I leave the main square.

Facebook reply comment from Sarah: "Finally you jumped." Text from Michael: "Guys' night, tomorrow!"

Guys' nights out are not subject to any rituals, planning, or duration. Some guys' nights out are over after just a few hours because there's nothing to say and it's not necessary to talk. Then there are guys' nights out that are wrapped up in the morning over breakfast.

I found out shortly beforehand that Sarah will be visiting me tomorrow. And I can briefly sum things up: SHE remains unreachable, which I find good in the meantime. Amy has returned to her boyfriend, dissatisfied with herself. And with Sarah, besides talking for hours, I can even have uncomplicated sex. I am satisfied. With exactly this mood in my belly, I am too early. I'm always too early. I am the one who is always ten minutes early at the meeting spot. I have no idea why, but I have always done that.

It is, of course, the place where I feel most comfortable or should feel most comfortable. I accept HER intrusion into my extended living room in the evening. The eyes are smaller than usual, the posture more crooked; one notices HER sadness. Perhaps it was too much of me. In any case, HER eyes avoid me today, and I am being ignored, which is probably better. *I'm a pig, after all!*

And so they roll in one after the other. David, freshly dumped, still slightly bruised, and slowly recovering. Chris, engaged—for the second time, but at least with the same woman—and, of course, Michael, newly in love and on the best path to live monogamously. Four men with different life stories, different points of view, and this is exactly what can make such an evening brilliant without the need to drink alcohol. After a short time, the conversation returns to women. And I am, unfortunately, the main target of the defamatory speech.

"How many women are you meeting now?" Chris asks, who doesn't seem to be up-to-date, so the grapevine doesn't seem to always work, which is good.

"Just one, that's enough. She's special."

"And the other nineteen?"

"Nineteen?!"

"Yeah, it's like a wine cellar with you. You drink one bottle and have nineteen in storage!"

Michael interjects, "And every now and then,

he opens several and has an orgy, and then has a thick head the next day!"

I try to interject, "Guys, we talked about monogamy not being perfect—monogamy is the issue."

"Can you even spell that?" David interjects, a big grin on his face.

I turn to Chris. "How does it feel to live monogamously?" but I immediately give myself the answer, "If the shoe fits, wear it!"

"Says the man who has consumed the life needs of a normal man in the last few weeks," David replies, grinning. A blonde is watching us. However, her golden retriever, which lies at her feet, ignores us.

"I only had sex once!"

"Once, twice, the same," Michael interjects.

"In the morning and in the evening," David adds.

I don't relish being the one everyone is picking on at the moment.

"Can you even store open wine that long?" adds Chris.

"She's sweet! It's an indescribable wine with a good aroma."

The atmosphere is loud, and we're already entertaining neighboring tables. Women's heads turn to us, some eyeing us with a grin, others turning away from us in disgust. SHE notices it—I feel it all at once. As I make my way to the restroom, SHE cuts me off.

"I was on vacation, I met a man, and imagine—he was nice, and I had a good chat with him. But some guy thought he wasn't good for me. In hindsight, maybe a good development, BUT how do you feel about others interfering in your life?"

48

"If it seems important, then you have to interfere."

"Even if it means hurting the other person badly?"

"I would do it without looking at the consequences. I would just do it." A pause, a moment too long occurs between the two of us, the sounds of guests are suddenly very far away, everyday life is removed.

"What is the real reason you left me?"

"I don't know anymore, but at this point, I think it was the right decision."

"You don't know. Great, then it must have been a really important reason."

"You're too old for me!"

"Oh, I thought the father of your child was only four years younger than me anyway?"

"You . . ." A tear begins to work its way down her face.

"I have to get back to work." She turns around and walks to her tables. As I continue on my way, I would love to vent my anger on anything. Get rid of my anger at myself. *I am an ass.* But the anger is absorbed into me!

"Did you arrange a date with her?" Chris asks with a grin, unaware that he has just stirred up a hornet's nest.

"No," escapes between pressed lips. Michael and David are frowning; Chris is clueless. I don't want to let him in on it either!

"How's the house construction coming along?" I try to steer the conversation in a new direction. Away from the serious topics to weather and other superficialities that make up the world, where you can talk for hours and yet say nothing about it.

"We received the full thermal protection these days!" Good, I managed; the next few minutes are about energy efficiency, good advice, what to look for, and where. Men who have already built houses— like ducks in the water.

Tomorrow, Sarah is coming. She'll already be in Linz for brunch. Where am I going to take her? What will the itinerary be? runs through my head as our conversation flows along.

"You are the social project of all of us!" Michael returns the topic to me. "After all, you're already sleeping with women you said you'd never sleep with because you don't want to ruin the friendly relationship between you two."

"Platonic relationships between men and women rarely work anyway, because one of them is always into the other," David adds.

"Great! Thanks for making me and my love life the topic today," I grin to the group.

"You don't have a love life—you have a business model," Michael shoots back and explains to the others my idea that I came up with the other day: driving women back to their ex-boyfriends/husbands when they go out with me!

"Ok, if this is the case—and you have proven this with examples in your recent past—then tell me about the ex-boyfriends of the current ladies in your address book."

Sometimes I think to myself, *I could strangle my friends.* I think about it for a moment and then try to remember.

"With HER, I don't know absolutely who the very last one was; I think SHE was a little bit more active in that respect. With Sarah, it's a man with whom she never got as far as to know if living together would work, and that nags at her still. Thus, a potential candidate," I explain with a wry smile on my face. My heart is pounding. I hate a pounding heart. My blood pressure is probably higher, too.

"She chokes to this day when she sees him!" I let my eyes drift across the room again, and know when I see HER face that she just doesn't forgive me. I remember my list that I wrote in the Cubus. Having a normal conversation would have been better back then. Just eye to eye, on neutral ground, no retreat for either of us. Only openness and then just be finished with it, but this way, I just hurt her. I tore the ground out from under her feet.

"HEY! What kind of daydream are you having right now with what woman?"

"With one who was important in my life! Cheers! Here's to one day focusing my energy on one woman worth having."

"I'll tell you one thing. Before you get married a third time, we're going to hit you over the head with a baseball bat. Just in case. So it hurts right from the start."

"Thank you for caring."

"That's what you have us for." David smiles back.

Text from Sarah: "Drunk? Where are your funny Facebook status messages?"

~~~

I have reached the summit—2,376 meters of altitude. The world lies at my feet, it lies below me. Michael, Frank, David, Karin, and Tina lie and sit with me, dispersed on the mountain. The sun is warm on this September day. We have risen 1,650 meters to the summit; we have climbed and mastered it via ferrata. All are sweaty and enjoying the silence, the calm, the cool breeze here at the summit with a magnificent view across the panorama. It is quiet up here; only the wind rustles softly on this last warm September day before the snow will come to the mountains.

During the ascent, we had stopped briefly at an alpine hut. An attractive—no, the most attractive hostess I have ever seen made me briefly think about what it would be like to work here as a host. Getting up well before six a.m. and defying wind and weather was enough of a disadvantage to drop the thought of continuing to flirt with her. Although, she had insanely long, attractive legs and a winning smile. I have to grin when I think about it.

Frank and Tina are cuddling in front of me. David writes texts to his possible new one. Michael and Karin are cuddling their way through their newly found love. I have to think briefly of Sarah's e-mails. The climb is where you have time to find yourself while enjoying nature.

Everybody is responsible for their own happiness. I remembered on the climb, and that SHE likes tattoos more. I wonder whether it's the same with Sarah. In any case, SHE likes such guys more. The kind that think "I am myself and I don't care what you want in the relationship!" It just sucks. I can't get HER out of my head. I'm sitting up here on the mountain and I have to think about HER, not about the hostess from before or the body of Sarah. No, about her. Damn. I only had one chance, and I blew it. I have seen her fifty-eight times in the last few months, and I saw one of my ex-wives, who also lives in Linz, exactly once in twelve years. This is exactly what makes me think, what distracts me from the beautiful view.

Only yesterday, I wanted to get bread at

Brandl bakery, and who of all people is no doubt standing behind me? When SHE sees me, there is no motion in the face. Maybe I hurt HER more if SHE sees me constantly in the city?

"Which of your chicks are you thinking about?" Michael throws at me. "Shouldn't you send them all a collective text?" I immediately discard the idea of throwing my sandwich at his head. I have identified the problem: SHE has not explicitly broken up with me, leaving such a wishy-washy conclusion that leaves all room for interpretation. Why can't a person in this day and age simply say, "IT IS OFF," state the reason, then close it as a memory? Single life is not as great as it might be imagined by a married man who thinks he is in a prison of his own making and craves freedom.

The sun is still intense today in this late summer. I close my eyes and try to absorb the peace of the mountain. This is exactly why I like climbing and hiking: the possibility to switch off, to come down. To let yourself drift. That's exactly why I like to sit on a peak. Ideally in the early morning, when the dawn dyes the mountain peaks a unique red.

Only today, it does not work. I don't get to rest; I can't push HER out of my thoughts and make room for others in my heart and head. Meanwhile, Michael looks at me doubtfully. Too long I have said nothing and looked mutely over him into the distance.

"Screw it," I say loudly so that all turn to me and rise, packing up the equipment. Karin, Michael's new girlfriend, would probably like to know why I just said that, but she doesn't dare to ask me yet. She might still be too shy in dealing with us as his friends.

The others, on the other hand, have known me for far too long to ask why I am talking to myself.

They won't know unless I want to tell them myself. However, I am beginning to worry about this habit.

The signal to leave was understood, and everyone stowed their provisions in their backpacks, tied their shoes, and began the descent. The goal of the leg: the hut with the snazzy hostess. The anticipation of a beer makes the men and the women move forward quickly. With the guys, I think it's also the landlady who makes them go faster. This could be a funny conversation at the hut overnight stay. Let's see how Karin deals with pretty women around Michael, especially when he unwraps his charm. For the first time in hours, I can grin again.

Men, simple-minded and hopelessly inferior to women as soon as we see long legs and a dazzling smile or the prospect of a good conversation. I wonder what Sarah is doing right now. Does she really see the whole thing as casually as I imagine? Can MAN hurt Sarah at all, and would Sarah and HER get along in bed? I stand still. What kind of thought was that? Ok, it is a widespread male fantasy, which is recognized as being overrated in reality, but Sarah and HER together in bed? Interesting . . . utopian. I need a beer.

Behind me, there is joking about the approaching men's vacation at Lake Garda. Tina tells Karin horror stories of the unproven activities we have allegedly engaged in when we take off once or twice a year for a long weekend. I see it as a kind of test for Karin to see if she can handle it. But she laughs and mocks Michael about the time when he once had to be carried home by us because his leg-brain coordination wasn't quite working anymore. If she only knew that it took us almost an hour to walk three hundred meters because our coordination was no longer in working order as well.

Lake Garda, climbing, hiking, and then a spa vacation in Austria with Sarah—what more could I want? I wonder if I should order a singer with flowers to her office or pay her a surprise visit. The surprise visit would undoubtedly be the better option. Do I still have the list on which I wrote down the possibilities to win HER back? Would this list also be used in case I had a girlfriend again and I lost her? Should I try one of the points again? Do I actually want to have HER back again in the meantime? Or are the fleeting real contacts in the city or the detailed Facebook comments enough? In the meantime, I have hidden the comments for me not to stumble over them twice a day because her profile is publicly accessible, and I catch myself rereading them. I should just ignore HER.

The advantage of constant brain-wanking is that time passes quickly, and an ascent that took about four hours flies by on the descent. The alpine hut is already close, and after several hours of sun on the rocks, you can smell the beer and the well-deserved roast pork from a distance.

It's nice to see Michael and Karin, newly in love, cuddled up close, waiting for dinner. But Frank and Tina's long-standing relationship hasn't suffered, either, and the two of them keep touching each other. David and I have stretched out our legs and are enjoying the sun without cuddling. Hanna, the hostess, runs past us again and again, and David and I get distracted again and again from looking at the wonderful mountain panorama.

The disadvantage of strenuous hikes is that the third beer is already two too many. Fatigue quickly takes hold of you; Karin and Michael have already disappeared. Tina fell asleep on Frank's shoulder, who just tries to stay awake. David and I are currently talking about all the world and his wife, interrupted only by the occasional buzz of David's cell phone.

"How can you write so many texts?"

No answer—just a grin on his face.

I enjoy not having thought about my women and my broken relationships for hours. I was supposed to become a monk—an evangelical monk living in a lonely alpine hut near Hanna's long legs.

I immediately discard the thought when I start to think of legs again and compare the length of Sarah's and Hanna's. This is especially easy for me right now because these legs are sitting next to me. One of her hands is on my arm, and she is having a great time with us. David is now telling Hanna the experiences that Tina already talked about today.

A little later, we put the two sleepyheads to bed. Nightfall is approaching. Somehow, Hanna looks at me as if she was still waiting for something from me as she stands in the doorway to her private rooms. Very briefly, I weigh my options. David looks at me and shakes his head, and he's right: it's better to be in camp with everyone than to leave something unfinished again. I have too many unfinished projects. Too many things that will keep me awake again. It's time to clear the decks. I nod to Hanna and have no idea what she is thinking. I turn around and drop onto the mattress.

No text on my cell phone. And no sleep again this night because I can't get Hanna's legs out of my head.

~~~

Guys' night out! Again! Once again! Wonderful! There was a group text by David and all are present. Everyone talks about this and that and, once again, using me as a social project is one of the main topics. Of course I am aware of the mistakes in my life, and it doesn't bother me when jokes are made about my two ex-wives or about the fact that I stockpile women like wine in the wine cellar and open one or the other at whim. And SHE is not present in the restaurant either.

But every now and then it's enough, so I decide in the spur of the moment—after I've finished my drink—to go to Sarah's place. I need my good friend now, the one who makes me feel comfortable simply being next to me.

"Mmhh. Hey—wow, what are you doing here? Anything happening?" she asks, puzzled. Apparently, she doesn't think it's such a great idea, though it seemed almost brilliant to me a few hours ago.

"I was at one of our men's meetings. Again, there was too much about me, and I just wanted to leave. All of a sudden, I was standing in front of your door."

A thoughtful and somewhat pondering look penetrates me. "You know, you should have called. I have a girls' get-together in fifteen minutes that involves drinking prosecco and gossiping until I drop. Maybe watching a DVD. Well, hang on."

She takes out her phone and dials, waiting for someone to pick up. "Hi, Sarah there. Is it ok if there is a man at our girls' get-together? My friend from Linz is there and somehow has problems with friends, women, and so on. Can't kick him out and don't know if he alone . . ." I feel stupid and strange right now.

Meanwhile, her eyes change to a grateful benevolent look.

"Thanks. Will you let the others know? See you in a bit." With that sentence, the conversation ends.

"What was that?"

Sarah explains to me that she is going to spontaneously take me with her and that her friend Karin, who just called her, thinks that it would be entertaining if I come along. "As a male perspective who can explain the male world to us." She will inform the other girls, but that should not be a problem. They know who I am from stories anyway.

"Can women be that uncomplicated?" I ask.

As an answer, there is only a raised eyebrow and a flash in her eyes followed by, "Come on, we have to go. Still have to get prosecco."

Finally, we find a spot to park. We go to the apartment of Karin, Sarah's friend, and I'm a bit excited—a girls' night out and me, the foreign intruder. I usually don't mind, but today I don't know anyone except Sarah. It's very exciting, as I've never met anyone from Sarah's crowd.

We ring the bell, and when the door opens, a friendly face is smiling at us. It is Karin. "Hi, come on in! Everyone's already here. Sarah, you know your way around, so take your friend and join the others. I'll get two more glasses and something to nibble on."

In the living room, four women—all very pretty, by the way—sit huddled together with cushions and blankets on the couch. They all greet us kindly. I introduce myself all around, and it seems like it's normal that I'm there. After some brief small talk so that we know the basics about each other, I go to the toilet to be alone for a while and to give the girls the opportunity to be alone. When I come back, the gossip about men is already taking place—you can always count on it with women. They don't seem to care that I'm a man they don't know and keep talking.

"I don't think it was just a sexual relationship. There was more—that's what I felt—but why the sudden end overnight?" Evidently, there was a breakup with Angelica. If I've been following this correctly, it was a while ago, but it still seems to be an issue.

"Look, we know you had extremely hot sex and you had numerous orgasms, but it's over now. He doesn't want to do it anymore; that's why he ended it. Obviously, he wants something else now, no matter what else was going on between you."

"He could have just been scared," I suddenly hear the words coming out of my mouth. Everyone turns to me, and Sarah's look scares me. Eyes that I have never seen before contain a mixture of loving understanding, joy, and warning.

"What was that?" Julia asks, astonished.

Stuttering a bit, I start, "Uhh, well—erm . . ."—I have to think of HER again for the first time in quite a while—"There are also men who are afraid. Afraid of too many feelings. We men know that there are feelings and they are brilliant, perfect, and great in the beginning, but they make things complicated with time. You put expectations on people that then might not be met, or you realize that you would hurt yourself over time."

"Such bullshit," Karin counters.

"It's true—a man's broken heart never heals properly or it lasts a lifetime, and if it's ever happened to a man, he keeps a safe distance. It could get too close, too dangerous, and someone would get hurt. He doesn't want that to be him, so he draws the line. It's stupid, but we think we're doing ourselves some good by doing this." Silence. No one says anything. *What did I do? Hello?*

"Yes, the poor men." An ironic comment from Sarah. It suits her. I have to grin.

Amazed about all the things I witnessed and how women talk about men and feelings, the evening ends after five hours. Topics like men, sex without feelings, sex with feelings, orgasm and orgasm difficulties, fidelity, cheating, sex toys, and so on were discussed. It could have gone on forever. It was fascinating to witness how the girls deal with each other, like a family that has warmly welcomed a new member. No one judging one another because of their views.

"It was great! I honestly enjoyed it. Thanks for the ride," I say to Sarah as we arrive at her home.

"Hope you had fun and it wasn't too boring. Hopefully you even understood a bit of Venusian?"

"Yeah, sure. You're just brilliant. So, I'm looking forward to bed . . ."

"You get the couch today. I'm just going to take a quick shower, and then you can go to the bathroom, ok?" Confused, I look around and try to think if she's messing with me.

Once home, she pulls me to her in the living room.

"Are you happy?" There's a look in her eyes that makes my smile freeze for a moment. I ponder.

"Yeees," I answer, clearly too distorted. "I am satisfied after all that happened to me during and after the divorce, satisfied—now!" She likes this answer better, and a friendlier smile flits along her face. "In itself, I feel happy. I have a family that supports me. A son who enriches my life here in Linz.

Friends who are there when you need them. The love life is not so important to me at the moment."

When I say the last sentence, I'm not so sure myself if I mean it the way I say it. I notice how she is processing; she is leaning back and then reaches for a pen. "Satisfied & happy" she writes on a piece of paper, pointing to the ampersand symbol.

"You are happy; you are satisfied. So the question is, are you happy AND satisfied?" Sarah lies on my back and points to the sign. She is naked. I can feel her breasts on my back.

"Actually, I didn't want to have sex with you!" And so now we lie on the bed while a starry night shimmers outside. Her hands are scurrying through my hair. Her scent is all over the room. I like that scent.

"I will be happy eventually. I have a few more things to take care of. Have to figure out this and that and bring some peace into my life. But I love that you exist!" Instead of a usual "ok," I get a kiss, and two long legs swing out of bed and disappear towards the bathroom.

"Why aren't you romantic, anyway?" I call after her, "And what if I wanted more?" I hear no more footfalls. Sarah usually paws around the apartment like a cat on soft soles.

"More?" she asks after what feels like an eternity of silence.

"I'm romantic!" the script quickly continues. When she returns, she smells even better, lying down next to me.

"We'll discuss my romance in a moment. First, I want to know why you don't know better? Because I don't understand you; you have everything you need." She beams at me.

"I feel that 'AND' too, but then again, what if it's not there anymore? When it's gone. I don't want to miss it again then." I pause.

"If I know, then I know, and you will know too," she finishes my thought and kisses me.

The room still smells like sex. Sarah has found her spot on my shoulder. If she starts purring now, it might become too romantic even for me. And suddenly, as she falls asleep, I think of the unanswered question she has dodged: "More?" She didn't just dodge it; she simply ignored it. *No way.* I stumble from one woman who doesn't know what she wants to the next who doesn't even share what she wants. My sleeping problems are back all at once. I can hear her breathing, and it's exactly this breathing that usually lets me fall asleep because I feel comfortable next to her, but tonight it keeps me awake and sounds leaden. A stone is suddenly on my shoulder. No SHE, no everyday problems; I suddenly have a problem with Sarah because I want more. Or I at least feel that way, and she's smoothly dodged it.

"Fuck that 'AND'," I mumble half aloud to myself. The night is done. I can hardly wait for the day to go home, or perhaps straight away? A look at the iPhone shows me no text, and I just do not feel like posting any Facebook status. What should I write anyway? Something to amuse the voyeuristic FB community, 80 percent of which I do not count among my friends at all. I try to turn around on the couch I know well by now, and I already know that this will be a long night.

~~~

Working days can have something calming about them. People always talk about separating private and professional matters and leaving your worries at home or not sleeping around at the office. Of course, I didn't stick to either of those rules.

It can happen that I take my luck or my troubles with me to the company, and when I say, "Never fuck in the office," there is a branch where I better don't show up without completely looting the adjacent flower store.

Anyway, there's nothing going on today. Nothing at all. The phone is silent; no e-mail is tangled in the inbox. Drinking the third coffee with my colleagues at ten o'clock, I write an e-mail to Sarah:

"My friends incl. girlfriends, even Benjamin, believe that there is love after all . . . I let myself think about it yesterday . . . not for me anymore . . . experienced too much . . . too many uncertain factors to go parachuting without a chute."

A short time later comes a response from Sarah; she probably has no patients right now.

"Love has ceased to exist? For you, anyway. LOVE, if we're honest, comes in different types, ways of looking at things, can be felt differently by every individual. You love your son and you love women in a different way, and when you are in a relationship, love also changes. From finding you nice, I like you, to being in love, to a deep love, which can then no longer be exciting but gives security. I think that you already believe in it, only you don't want to fall in love anymore and hurt yourself. If it fits, however, you can't always steer it the way you want; maybe you'll miss something, who knows, maybe the time will come again."

I answer back immediately.

"I know myself, I'll surely miss it! But I also have absolutely no idea, I don't have and don't know any magic formula . . . and I have . . . hmmm . . . who knows what I have . . . I only know one thing . . . I'm very lucky to have few good friends. And of course you too."

Sarah responds five minutes later.

"Just pay a little more attention to what's going on in your life. Enjoy what you have and try not to consciously block good things in your life. If you know when you're making mistakes, it's easier to pay attention to them. Keep your eyes open! ;-) Maybe you'll allow something into your life more often, even though you should leave it out. Because something is already there anyway, and you should spend your time on it."

I think about it for a moment while my colleague stares at me and surely feels sorry for me because of the abruptly appearing work.

"I'm certainly not blocking anything good! At least I let you in a bit :-) Besides, I need my corners and edges! I mean, with a woman . . . Don't you want to open a surgery in Linz? Kiss you, for being there."

This time Sarah takes longer, although I'm more eager for her answer.

"Everyone has corners and edges, but then they also fit together . . . and also that . . . do YOU want . . . who knows, maybe I'll take a day off and come to Linz. Pay you a visit . . . when I'm asked??"

A phone call prevents me from an immediate answer.

"With me, you will become rich! Tell you what . . . sometimes I wish to go back to my school days, when I was shy, looked ugly and didn't just blabber on and was cheeky and just took what I felt like . . . it had advantages just to dream about it . . . and not to dream and put it into practice . . . I have been wondering about something completely different in the last few weeks . . . I have 2 exes . . . they don't want to have anything to do with me anymore . . . because I . . . can also be really mean, or it is perceived that way . . . but the rest . . . the rest . . . I have the feeling that they always want to know how I'm doing as if they had taken me to their hearts . . . in a sick way . . . interesting . . . e.g. Amy . . . she keeps contacting me in some intervals (at least until recently)! Or a girl from Cologne, whom I once 'knew,' who also regularly writes an e-mail."

Again, Sarah takes her time. Lunch time is already approaching; I will skip my lunch once more.

"You and your women. I don't understand why you sometimes still look for contact. At some point you wrote that you had broken everything off. Now you don't. Sometimes you have to take a decision. Decide for yourself what you want and then act on it. :-) you are as you are! Whether you can even stand a few days alone with me in the spa without other women . . . doubtful."

Sarah is simply unique in her own way. Unfortunately, she lives so far away.

"I HAVE . . . canceled . . . but I certainly do not change mobile numbers, e-mail addresses, and the rest!!! :-) AND YES . . . I can get along for months with only you . . . probably for years. I am certainly not actively looking for contact . . . but I also certainly do not say NEVER WRITE ME AGAIN . . . I'm not like that, I have no problem with them! . . . why should I . . . I don't want anything from them . . . so . . ."

Sarah replies again and makes me thoughtful.

"And if you don't react at all?? ;-) I'm curious

. . . in case we really go to the thermal spa . . . :-)"

With that, I let her have the last word; she has earned it with her clear, direct manner. I lean back and try to think about what kind of work I could be doing so that I don't have to think about what I've written.

~~~

HER Facebook entry: "Does love always hurt so much?" I avoid giving my opinion. I could not do that anyway. I'm just stalking her. I suffer. I think I have to suffer.

I should actually break off contact. "So I'm thinking in conditionals again," I whisper to myself.

Wasn't there once a saying by a friend that one needs half of the time spent in a relationship to forget? Because if so, this information urgently needs to be evaluated; despite the short time, I'm still hanging on to HER. And then there's the example of my ex-wife with whom I have had no contact for years who still hates me.

So the time period just doesn't fit.

~~~

"You must be cheating," Tina interjects as her husband goes on again about how we visited Andre Heller's botanical garden at Lake Garda.

Sarah, snuggled against my shoulder, moves. "The ten guys must have arranged that story to distract from their alcohol excesses with it." The ladies in the group nod in agreement while we men protest loudly. In all the commotion, the laughter, the half-hearted assurances, Sarah beams from the crowd. She immediately blended into the group of my friends. Even Benjamin, who plays with the children, must have taken her into his heart. She was taken in and could immediately talk about us and the men's vacation on Lake Garda.

"Cultural sightseeing without women? Don't make me laugh." Denise punches her husband in the side. "If I had been there, you wouldn't even have known who Andre Heller was." My sister, Mary, grins knowingly at her husband at this remark.

But it's true: We were really there, and we hadn't had a single night out before. Well, perhaps that's not true for everyone . . . actually, we were only four of us, and yes, I was there. "How was it when you found your pants in the hotel pool early that morning?" Mary laughs at me, and my brother-in-law immediately tells the story of why my pants were floating in the pool that morning.

One thing we men swore to each other at that time was to tell everything at home. Because with ten men, nothing stays secret, and the partners know each other much too well for that. I have to grin at my sister.

"It was the most relaxing vacation you could have with nine other men."

"Waking up without professional appointments, trouble at work, or children who you can hear laughing as they jump into bed to start the day much too early," Michael interjects, and so the conversation sways back and forth as we enjoy the last remaining hours of sunshine outdoors on this beautiful fall day.

Sarah's eye color changes depending on her mood, I notice at this moment. When she jokes, it's an emerald green. "How are you actually doing with our lovely Casanova?" Denise asks Sarah. Suddenly, it's there, that silence where you would hear even an earthworm eating its way through the soil.

Sarah sits up, stretches her back, and the color of her eyes changes—is it a blue now? "He is peculiar, as you all know. He has a weird history that might take some getting used to and his own way of dealing with the present. How he plans his future is still a mystery to me, but one thing is clear: He can't handle money."

A brief pause makes the silence unbearable as my sister tilts her head and looks at Sarah more closely as she continues speaking. "Let me put it another way: A woman gets used to being considered a toy but does not tolerate it and presents herself as a toy with rough edges. Then, the little children quickly let go. He who can handle it will touch it in the right places. He can touch right. Now, if he didn't brain-wank so much, he would be almost perfect."

I have to repeat the last sentences a second time in my head to understand them while my sister is already beaming broadly. *Women simply grasp complex entities faster, but in return, we decide faster,* my ego races after this thought.

Emerald green eyes shine at me and whisper in my ear, "You are just you." She then immediately follows up with, "I think he has discarded the Casanova life—at least for the time being."

Who would not like this woman? I think to myself at this moment. The women nod as if they all knew me well and meanwhile their men surely think of the time at Lake Garda where ten men only planned from hour to hour in an uncomplicated way and spent most of the time in trattorias only to fall into bed sober at a later hour. Well, almost all—more precisely—some, and they were not strictly sober, and yes, of course, I was always there.

Facebook status: "Arrived home!"

Surprisingly, some like that.

~ ~ ~

It's a Monday morning. I'm sitting at work, and the phone is ringing all the time. At the moment, there is a lot going on because the system has collapsed. *Too much is too much*, I think to myself, and I go to grab a cup of coffee. The world doesn't end if I'm not available for five minutes. I enjoy the sound of the coffee machine while the coffee pours into my cup. This time, I used a golden capsule. I wonder what these big companies earn with such mini capsules in various colors. *No—stay focused and go back to the desk. Continue to radiate peace, be an IT nerd, and pretend to have everything under control.*

A glance at my cell phone. A missed call. It's eight a.m.; who wants something from me? Sarah. "Hi, you. And how are you?" she asks.

"If I'm honest, it's very hectic right now. The system has broken down, and everyone wants something from me. I haven't been in such demand and so highly requested in a long time."

Laughing, she replies, "I want something from you, too. This coming weekend will be a relaxing weekend at the spa. I have already booked something in advance. What do you say?" Sarah just knows me so well. Meanwhile, we have been together more or less for weeks. The casual story has turned into a very solid relationship where even in the evening we just talk or watch TV. It works. She can hear what I think. Just like now—I have so much work to do, which I would never admit to, and I need an urgent break.

"I'm in. You're a sweetheart." *Welcome to the*

relationship trap. Soon, she redecorates my apartment.

A new spa you've never been to is always exciting. You have to explore the whole area and take it all in. I still enjoy seeing Sarah looking at things and just smiling because she doesn't realize anyone is watching her. We check in and go to the room to unpack and change for the spa. Worn out from the car ride, I lay down on the bed. A few seconds later, I feel the bed shake as she comes to me on the bed and gives me a kiss, gently and very soulfully. Like almost every time, my whole body tingles.

The weekend at the spa is brilliant. Pure relaxation with whirlpool baths, a sauna, massages, cozy dinners, wonderfully exciting TV evenings in bed, and philosophizing about all the world and his wife. We have found a proper ritual. First, sauna; preferably the herbal sauna, which is not too hot, but it smells wonderfully of balm and fir, and if you look at the wooden ceiling of the sauna, colorful little lights shine. There are endless different colors. Red, blue, orange, green, and yellow. I found out that every thirty seconds, the colors change from blue to green, then yellow, orange, and red. Always the same sequence. When I'm not looking at the lights, I'm watching Sarah. How she lies there with pleasure and is breathing in peace. The belly always moves slowly up and down. Quietly and regularly. Of course, we talk to each other until the others in the sauna are upset. It has a good effect, though, because we have the sauna to ourselves at the end and when we are alone, I can also touch her. I just like to "experience" her. After the sauna, it's off to the little whirlpool and then resting with a book or a little nap on the big double lounge chair. If one didn't have to work, I would stay here forever. I want more with her.

As I go to post a Facebook status, I realize she has turned off my smartphone.

What a woman.

~~~

Cafés have their positive and, of course, negative sides. On the one hand, you're alone among an unknown crowd that continuously changes stories and faces; on the other hand, you can feel lonely and lost.

I like the feeling of observing. The stories of the people sitting at the table, what moves them at that moment. How they relate to their neighbor, whether it's a business or personal conversation. Like right now, at the next table where the father is trying to go for a coffee with the teenage son. The son he only sees weekly. And his only effort at this moment is to reprimand the son as to why he is not doing his homework. The father worries that his son will not complete the task set for him in time. The son just doesn't want to, for whatever reason; I know myself what kind of ideas and thoughts I had in my head at that time as a teenage boy. But still, the father helps, and the son writes along, lost in thought. It's a good thing that there are smartphones. "You could have already done it during the week. Now you're stressed again this weekend!" And then those pauses where words and actions matter. *Just leave him alone and enjoy the few hours you have with him,* I think to myself. *And make up for his mother's lack of homework,* pops into my head.

I think cafés are marvelous.

I send Sarah a text: "I know you're working, but I've taken the day off. I'm sitting in a café watching people. Do you want to share my observations?"

I watch for a while how the weekend daddy cares for his son and means well with him, and how the son just doesn't want to do homework. I have to think of my son still striving in school, not yet despairing for his school achievement. Soon, he will have other interests, and then I, too, will probably be anxious for his future in the rare time we have amid all the temptations that exist at this time. I'll be allowed to fetch him again in a moment.

The clock is approaching the noon hour; it is time to leave, to get him. How long will he like this, leading two lives? Eleven days with his mother, then two nights with his father. He has been under tremendous strain for years. I admire him for that and also hope at the same time that it doesn't leave too much severe damage to his psyche and that he can eventually start a relationship without prejudice.

"Where do we meet?" a woman suddenly shouts into her phone. "I'll take the train, then!" A short pause—everyone in the room is curious about the solution. "No, you will have to pick me up at the platform!" I grin. I love watching people.

As I pay, my phone vibrates. Sarah leaves me a short message, apparently too stressed out to engage in longer texting. Too bad; I would have liked to share with her my meandering thoughts. The observations of the day. But that's how it is when you try to have a monogamous relationship with a woman whose sobriety in relationship questions is sometimes too close to reality. I think of the saying of a friend: "If you don't have love in your heart, you don't have anything." I must talk to Sarah about these words on occasion . . . not that she has only a stone left for me instead of a heart. And at that moment, I realize that she is just like that. She has always been like that. Cool in relationship matters. Objective about her feelings. And that's how I met her. That's exactly how the feelings deepened, even though I still occasionally look around for a woman on the street. Like just now, I look after this long-legged, black-haired woman and forget her at the same moment.

I should get a new outfit, it suddenly occurs to me. *As long as I can still decide freely.*

"Shopping tour through Linz," I find appropriate as a status now.

~~~

Completely tired after a long working day, I come home. I empty the mailbox and go upstairs to the apartment. Brochures are thrown away, as usual, without bothering to look at them. A letter from the lawyer—one of the ex-wives probably wants more money, or someone is suing me for child support for a child I didn't know about. But it's just an invitation to a lecture that I am no longer interested in just by reading the headline. Then a letter with my name, my address—handwritten—from I don't know who. No sender. The letter is opened. Somehow, I'm pleased, finding it exciting and thrilling. I scan a few pages—also handwritten—and look to see who is listed at the end. A name—a woman's name: Sarah. *Sarah?*

Why is she writing me a letter? I wonder. I get myself something to drink just to be on the safe side. For whatever reason, I have a bad feeling. Bad memories come up. When was the last time I saw her—about ten days ago? Until now, I didn't even know what her handwriting looked like; apart from e-mails and texts, we didn't communicate in writing. And telephoning, as you know, works orally.

Very well. It says:

Hey, As you probably noticed, our contact has been a bit dull lately. We haven't heard from each other or written to each other that often, and the visits have become less frequent over the last few months. I didn't respond at all last weekend because I needed time.

Time for me to think about myself, my life, 'us' (or something like that), and everything related to that. The situation that on the one hand I am your good 'platonic' friend—as you call me—with whom you can do anything and everything, tell her everything, visit your friends, take trips together, and on the other hand, the fact that this has changed in the meantime is difficult. Difficult for me.

On the one hand, you tell me about your life, your friends, your women—what you do, want to do, who you meet, your friends, your son, and so on. You share your life with me in such a way that it becomes too much for ME. And you kept your status on Facebook set to single.

We both said at first that it was just something 'casual,' but over time—almost a year now—it has changed. Things change. There are different kinds of relationships and one of them is what we have. Yeah, you don't want to hear that, and you don't want to have that because you don't want to get hurt anymore and you don't want to fall in love properly. That's fine and I understand that. I can really understand that.

I will really miss you a lot because you became part of my life. As of now, though, I want my life back to myself.

Please do not contact me! No calls, no e-mails, no flowers, no chocolates, no 100 attempts that you

write down first—just nothing. Thank you!
LOVE . . . Yours, Sarah

I am speechless. Everything was so great just a few days ago. We had great conversations and felt good. Cuddled, had fun. It was so . . . so familiar. Although, she was different. One moment or another, it was more distant than usual. Did Sarah plan this and already know she was ending it with us? With "us"—sounds somehow quite normal. I smirk in pain. Am I that blind? Don't I recognize any signs anymore?

Well, even if I'm not supposed to get in touch, I'll call Sarah. After a letter like that, I'm allowed to give feedback, right? It's my right!

Pressing quick dial key #2. Connection is established. The phone rings. My heart is beating. Why is it suddenly beating like that? Because I'm nervous? Because I'm afraid she won't answer the phone, or am I fearful that Sarah has disappeared from my life? No one's picking up. I don't know what to do right now. I take my phone and call David, and we meet an hour later at the local pub. We order a bottle of red wine. It's just part of the package now.

"Did something happen? Sounded like it on the phone," he asks me. At the moment, I don't know what to say. *Did something happen at all? What should I do? Sarah is gone and I don't want that.* These sentences run through my confused brain. From beginning to end, the Sarah story is rolled up, and I tell him about the letter. "What do you actually want to know from me now?" he continues to ask.

"Oh, I don't know. I feel like something is being taken away from me. It was a casual story—maybe a little different from all the other women, but I didn't want it to end like this. I don't want to lose

Sarah, but I'm not supposed to or allowed to come forward. What should I do?"

David's look changes, and he starts to speak. "Look, you've been through a lot with different women, as we know, including your two ex-wives. We know that a man's broken heart never heals completely and has its scratches, but you can't keep blaming new women in your life for it. You should think about what exactly it was with Sarah." A short pause, which my dear friend uses to take a sip of the red wine. "Think about it—you haven't been seeing another woman in over a year. You only talk about her; there's only Sarah in your life. Yes, she doesn't live in your town, but that's not an insurmountable obstacle. You have a relationship, or had one. Everyone saw that, except you and her. You should think about that before you do anything rash." Now I take my glass of wine and take a sip; I'm speechless right now. It only happens rarely, but I repeat to myself again the spoken sentences I heard.

"Mmhh . . . yes, maybe," I answer and change the subject. I will think about it when I am alone. On the other hand, I see with David that luck exists. His new girlfriend is in harmony with him and I bet they will marry soon. I wouldn't be surprised, at the rate they're going.

This weekend, I decide to hide in my apartment. Phone off, computer off. Everything is turned off. I sit down on the couch and think about my life. What do I want? What do I want now and what do I want for the future? I haven't really thought about it that much. At least not since HER. With HER, I would have wanted to have everything.

Dream girls have the habit of becoming a reality.

I repeat her name. *Sarah.* I lost her, and no,

that's not something that needs to be shared with all of fucking humanity.

~~~

I didn't see the blow coming. I remember after I didn't catch Sarah on the phone, I was out the door to drive to her place, to offer her a word like the sissy I am right now. Then I was at the elevator, then there was this arm with the snake tattoo, and then it was dark too.

I'm lying in the hospital. I've been half awake for a few minutes already, having recalled the scenes before my blackout over and over again, and as I slowly wake up, I feel the presence of people in the room. A brief flash of thought makes me remember the admission, the blaring horn, the lights in the hallway, quiet voices asking me about something, and then there was nothing.

The nurse looks at me disapprovingly and surely thinks to herself, "Thug." No wonder—when I look in the mirror, a swollen left half of my face shines at me in all colors. My first thought goes to Benjamin, the second to Sarah, and the third to the snake. "We're even, even if it took months with you," I mumble into my numb cheek and earn another disapproving look from the nurse. The first impression with her has gone completely wrong.

"The police will then question you later about why you were lying bleeding in the stairwell."

These are exactly the kind of days a person wants to have. A severe headache, a face shimmering in all colors, and the police already waiting outside the room. I didn't even notice when I woke up that my sister was standing in the room.

"Well, didn't I tell you that one day someone

would smack you?"

Because her voice is similar to our mother's, at that moment it sounds like both of them are reprimanding me.

"Do things always have to break with you before something better can follow? By the way, you look terrible, and I'm glad you woke up." She speaks and hugs me at the same time. If my head didn't hurt, it would be a sentimental hug. She looks at me with her wet eyes.

"I know who did it, but it was just a punch; we're even. I made him look a bit ridiculous. But that he waited so long to do it?"

My sister is still waiting for a more detailed explanation, which I refuse to give her.

"Why?"

"Because I'm me, impulsive and not always thinking about what I'm doing. Sometimes I just don't think about the consequences."

"That's not an explanation for me!" she probes further.

"A few months ago, there was a billboard at the foot of the Pöstlingberg—maybe you passed it once—where someone was smooching a woman," I start to explain. "Well, he wasn't kissing his girlfriend at the time, and I took the picture and stuck it on the billboard. He was on the way home from being with his girlfriend, who probably saw this and broke up with him."

My sister can look disapproving in a way all her own, but now I'm earning that look.

"See, it's exactly because of that look that I didn't tell you about this."

"Why on earth did you do that? What business is a stranger's life of yours?"

At this very point, I could tell her that in the

deepest abysses of my soul, I hoped to regain HER. That SHE would flee into my arms with tears in her eyes. Instead, SHE gave me a disparaging knowing look that I didn't sleep for days because of and scowled at everyone. But I kept silent.

"I had my reasons." I don't want to have this discussion with my sister—my head hurts too much right now for that.

Thanks to the police arriving at this moment, I am saved from having to provide further explanations.

"Police Inspector Koller. Good day!" a civilian of about thirty years of age greets me formally. He has a firm handshake. I introduce him to my sister and ask him to take a chair. "After you were found unconscious and bloody in the hallway outside your apartment, we would like to know how this happened and if you might know who beat you up?"

"Uh . . ." An *uh* escapes me, the hint in rhetoric that the defendant is just trying to talk his way out of something. The *uh* covers the pause while the brain needs to put the words in the appropriate order.

"Uh," I repeat to myself, "beaten up? Excuse me, but I think I rather ran into the door full force because I thought it was still open, and then I probably hit my head too hard on the stone."

The look on my sister's face is unspeakably serious. The policeman, on the other hand, seems superficially disinterested, presumably having seen through me at the first '*uh*'.

"So, you want to explain that you fell as a result of an accident?"

"The way you put it sounds perfect. I don't know who would have wanted to beat me up, and I would certainly have seen or noticed something. But

I forgot something, got angry about it, then turned around and wanted to open the door, which was probably already closed again. I can't tell you exactly. But I know I believe that I was not beaten," I lie to him with a tortured, colorful face.

"That's good—it saves us a lot of work," Mr. Koller explains while getting up. "If you think something else happened to you, I would ask you to call this number." He hands my sister a card, says goodbye, and leaves.

"You lie without blushing."

"You can't say that. I just saw myself in the mirror; my face has several colors, including red," I try to grin.

My sister shakes her head and looks at me. "I was worried. What if he does that again?"

"He won't. I hope so, at least; the matter is settled, and we both will stick to the story, especially towards the parents, that I was just too clumsy. That shouldn't be too hard. I really hit the door head-on once, but luckily it was open at the time."

This time, my sister smiles slightly.

"Does Benjamin know about this?" I try to change the subject.

"Yes, I called him earlier. He will be taken here for a short time by his mother. He just knows that you had an accident." In my mind, I thank my sister for that—for being my sister.

"You know, I don't always make life easy for myself, especially in my love life! I seem to like it when things get a little more complicated. I'm probably the one who likes to make things complicated, too. Despite that, I'm satisfied, even if it ended with Sarah."

"You and Sarah are no longer a couple?"

"That's the question. Were we ever a couple at

all? Or, rather, another chapter in the never-ending story of Friendship Plus? I don't know, but in any case, she ended it in writing. And I have to admit, the fallout yesterday didn't encourage me to try it again, now that I think about it. She didn't answer the phone, and I'm certainly not texting her that I'm in the hospital. I know her; she wants no more contact now. I could do what I want. Maybe she's looking around for a sophisticated doctor."

I have to grin as my sister looks at me questioningly.

"When I used to know her in passing, I always felt like she was in a relationship with the whole world, meaning in multiple relationships." Whenever my sister tilts her head to a disapproving look, it becomes dangerous. The look penetrates me as there is a knock.

"DAAAAAD!" my son comes storming through the door. I catch his mother with a glance as the door slams shut; she remains standing outside in the hallway. She and I really have nothing to say to each other.

"Can you give me a gentle squeeze? My face hurts."

"How did that happen?" is the first question my son asks, followed by dozens more. I hesitate briefly, wanting to give him the explanation that I clumsily ran into the door and continue to hesitate. Silently, I look at him and think of my silent promise to him never to lie to him for no reason.

"You know, I hurt someone very badly, because my pride was hurt. Because I thought I was too important. So, that person smacked me, and I took an unfortunate fall and hit the ground. I also know that this person will be sorry afterward for having acted in such a way. I know one thing for myself: I will never again do such a thing as I did then. I will think about the consequences beforehand, and I will tell my parents in the same way." I look at my sister, who nods in agreement.

"So you lost the fight!" says Ben.

"Uh, yeah, but he was also taller than me by a head."

"Dad, you need to train more." Kids have their own views on various subjects, and just now, he found out that his dad lost a fight. Black and white. Genius.

Ben stays there for a few minutes until he says goodbye and is whisked back outside by his mother.

"Thank you!" I yell after a closing door. My sister is still sitting by my side.

"Mom, Dad?"

"Coming later." And with that, we both sink into a short while of silence, during which the sobriety of the room affects me. I notice that although there are three beds here in the room, I am alone with my sister.

Alone. In itself, every person is alone. Alone with his thoughts and the wishes he holds back in order not to frighten his partner. Alone when he dies. And even more alone when a person leaves him with whom he could communicate well.

"Should I call her?" I ask half aloud to myself. My sister glances at me.

"I don't know her that well, but knowing her, she will have told you what she definitely *doesn't* want. So weigh it out. Because I know one thing: You always leave a mark on someone's life. Whether it's good or bad, that's another question, but if you've made a good impression, time will tell." Occasionally, my sister can even be kind with her looks.

"I never really loved Sarah, because she didn't want to be loved, and I didn't let her, because no one can be loved who doesn't let themselves." With the sentence that superficially satisfies me, I try to bring the conversation to an end.

Minutes of silence, of being introverted, are abruptly interrupted by the loud intrusion of David and Michael, who grin at the sight of me and ask how this could have happened. They represent more radical positions than Benjamin, mock me as a wimp with a grin, and make it clear that at some point, one of the cuckolds would "choke" me.

Instead of them avenging me, I think to myself. My sister listens quietly, partly shaking her head, then reacts again with a laughing face to the dialogue that sways back and forth without regard for my aching face.

It is nice to hear in their undertone that they are glad that nothing more has happened, and that's why I get mockery and ridicule. One more story, which will be gladly unpacked in a wine mood one day and rubbed in the face of my current woman.

I spare myself to post it on Facebook; a son and two friends who laugh at me are enough.

When the topic of me and women comes up, my sister adds, "The perfect one! This says everything, and how everything is wrong in today's time anyway. We recently had a lecture on the subject of genitals and contraception in our professional training. The lecturer said that we live in a society that is oversexed, and that what is really important falls by the wayside. It takes away what is special about the act of love. And you, brother, have already gone off the track."

Silence. I look briefly at my upper arm, notice my scar, and think of that one night and of HER.

Then I look my sister in the eye again.

My sister can be a real buzzkill sometimes, getting to the point with a few sentences. I skim over my cell phone in the moment of pause. Twenty-one unread messages. I don't feel the urge to read them, but I see that Amy is among them.

~~~

The advantage of Vienna is that a few friends have come here over the years. But that's about it. However, it is enormously convenient to stay there after a rare opera evening if one would go to the opera, which happens to me twice in a decade. The friendships are sometimes deeper and then again more superficial. Now and then, a text or a phone call gets lost, but it's more common to stay in touch via Facebook. Laura was surprised when I called her and was thrilled to have been chosen as a refuge to disappear with for a few days into the anonymity of a larger city.

Alex would have offered himself, but Alex and his nihilistic attitude towards women and relationships would probably have pulled me down even more. Plus, my face still hurts, and I don't want to hear any stupid jokes there either. Laura is an acquaintance from the wild times who moved from a small town to a big city. From a small town to a cosmopolitan city—at least for the Viennese.

She is perfect as a place of refuge. For me, she is asexual, and that means something with a stewardess. I will at least try to persuade myself about that. She's not a special drinker who would drag me around pubs for hours, nor a chatterbox like Sarah, who I could listen to forever as she talked incessantly. I also don't need a family connection at the moment, and certainly no hormone-filled single men. I just need to get away from home. It happened incidentally that I saw HER when I left the hospital, a bouquet of flowers in her hand, as she was entering the hospital. A quick nod from both sides and the moment was gone.

And so, I ring Laura's doorbell with a Linzer torte under my arm, hoping that this evening will not end as emotionally as the last time I sought refuge with Sarah. I should have perhaps visited Alex after all.

I am aware that a similar situation happened not long ago, but I feel emotionally up to it, because I do not want to experience it again.

Opening the door, a slim, size XS black-haired woman stands in front of me with alert eyes and a laughing mouth. She is dressed casually—unusual for Miss Styled—and beams at me. *Haven't seen her for far too long,* goes through my head. However, she has no towel wrapped around her. Women who are not in a relationship with me are happy when they see me. No everyday conversations. No standard relationship life that restrains one. Something is lost then on the way to a partnership with me.

She squeezes me, sizing up the Linzer torte with a calorie-trained eye, and seconds later I'm gently pushed into the couch. Once again, a couch, once again in a woman's apartment, and once again she is comfortably dressed. But this time, I certainly won't touch her. No massage—just stay on the couch and see her as a neutral being.

"How was the well water?" I don't know my way around for a few seconds, rummaging through my memories. Any behavioral psychologist would have a field day with my eyes rotating in my face.

When she starts to help me, I remember the Facebook entry.

"I haven't tried it, and the well wouldn't be that deep. But thanks! I have to stop sharing everything on Facebook." I grin at her.

"What's going wrong in your life again now? Look at you; your face is glowing with different colors right now—what truck did do this to you?" After a week of recovery at home, you can still see the traces of the knockdown on me. It was two weeks of recovery. No Internet, little television. Only profound music that kept me in my lethargy.

"Short version: in love, heartbroken, screwed around, met other women again, maybe fell in love again—or was it an upset stomach? I don't know the difference with butterflies anymore. Then I embarrassed the lover of the previous one, who then laid one on me," I point to my face, "climbed around in between—on mountains, of course. Is that enough?"

"No!" Short pause.

"I have wine here, a comfy couch, nibbles, and endless time. Until Wednesday, to be exact, when I have to fly again. And I like hearing your stories about how you haven't missed a beat for years to show us all that you can experience anything and leave nothing out."

"Yeaaah," it comes out drawn out as I think, *Yes, Sarah*. "How are you?"

"You asked for asylum, so it's your turn. But in short, since the last time we had coffee together, nothing earth-shattering has happened. Vienna is a city full of misogynistic men. At least you are still sympathetic. So, I still haven't found my dream man, and as long as I don't find him or he doesn't find me, I won't look at any man, not even as a sample. Do you still go to your regular place?" Why can women, without so much as twitching the corner of the mouth, just change the subject with one sentence?

"Certainly, five times in a month. The cheeseburgers, in the meantime, have become a fixed part of my evening diet. I need at least one vice that I could give up at a doctor's check-up. It's just been my favorite place for almost twenty years now."

"Yeah, I guess you've found a food hub for yourself there."

"Hmmm. A pub as a center of life. But it's true. Friendships were deepened, love was found, drinks were had, people were met," I grin weakly at her.

A fixed point in my life is this Exxtrablatt, my regular pub. A resting place, the starting point of nightlife for me. The grin of Hari, the boss, who seems to know everyone personally. A handshake alone and everyday life is forgotten, or at the latest when I get the cheeseburger on the table. If I get a table at all.

I look at her for a long time in silence, and for the first time in my life, I don't necessarily see a sex object in an unattached woman. A toy for my EGO. Across from me sits a woman who is a friend—actually the same as Sarah or Theresia who was just before HER. Whose evenings I enjoyed, whose ideas enriched me and made my life entertaining, and I destroyed our friendship through sex. Destroyed it when feelings came into play that I didn't want to reciprocate. I could not. Because I was an ass on the EGO trip. If only I had never started it with Sarah.

"Where the hell are you with your thoughts again? You're sitting there grinning one second and being serious the next. What's on your mind right now?"

"Hmm . . . too much, as usual, and especially

the realization that I really am empathically abusing, abusing women as playthings of my ego. Maybe as a hunting trophy, keeping them until I get bored with them or don't want to get emotionally involved at all."

"Yes, sometimes you give the impression of being a player. One who gives gifts to the other and cares about the person, only to hurt them unconsciously or consciously the next day. But do not worry; you have also managed that with me. When I needed help, you were there, only to tell me when a feeling emerges that you are just fucking with another. By the way, the cake tastes good," she says and cuts off the third piece. And through her slow chewing, no more emotion is visible on her face. "And you had too many girlfriends. That scares a woman away! Maybe cross that out when introducing yourself to a new one. Believe me, that doesn't go down well, to feel like number xy." It comes out barely understandable between chews.

"You know, not so long ago, I sat with Sarah on the couch for the same reason. The lack of understanding on my part of how and why women think and act. May I show you something?" I look on my cell phone for a photo that I have had there for some time. It's a text I received once: "I increasingly have the feeling that I don't love you enough and that you feel the same way."

"I just don't understand that once there's a crisis, it's always over for you in this I'm-going-to-blow-it-all-away world. Why must only the feeling be constantly questioned? Why does a woman no longer live?" Well, at least her mouth remained open. Now, while eating, there's a tiny bit of food residue in the upper left corner by the incisor.

Shall I tell her? No, I allow myself this

triumph now and have something to smile about.

I ignore the fact that my smartphone has already announced itself for the second time, and we continue our discourse. When it reports the third time, I look graciously.

"I am now in a relationship again—with Manfred, a man with whom I had a liaison shortly before you :-) . . . You should push your idea as a business model. Miss your humor, Sarah"

I show it to Laura wordlessly. Her laughter lasts for minutes while I remain speechless at the table and then explain to her the business model with the ex who becomes number one again. Such evenings are not for the faint of heart. On the other hand, they are the salt in the soup of life—my life. I can't even be mad at Sarah, because I know that it didn't hit me that deeply.

"You know, sometimes I feel sorry for your lost soul!"

"What soul?"

"The one you buried deep inside, thinking it would never come back," Laura says, looking at me with a serious look.

"How was your shopping trip?" she follows up. A brilliant change of subject.

"I was at H&M, Peek, Boss. Only the shoes—"

"*Fashion* at H&M? Since when do they have fashion there?"

"Underpants."

"Oh, underpants, that currently no one sees you in anyway," she grins.

"But I am a weapon in a suit, dangerous and hot," I try to retort.

"You? Impossible! In the end, it's only . . . you!" She wins. "Besides, a slingshot is also a weapon but not hot. Even a telephone book can be a weapon;

a woman can kill people with it. In that respect, you are a phone book: ponderously thick," she humiliates me further.

"Because I'm so appealing," I try again, "and incomprehensible, unmanageable, and above all, nobody needs it because we all have the Internet anyway." I give in and laugh along.

Then she turns to me. "Do you know what I would like to be one day?"

"Queen?"

"No, you dork. I'd like to be the wife for a man one day who thinks that I would have been THE one. I mean for a man to sit there in his old age and think to himself, that woman—me—would have been it." Her look is sad.

I am not alone in the world carrying my pack on my back. Later, as I sit back, I feel different.

"I should delete the Facebook account . . . Am I being too nice?"

"Sometimes you make it too easy for a woman. Sometimes you don't have any edges. But you're still you, and that's why I like you. And now I'm going to bed. The couch is for you, you manly wimp."

"What do you think about the following status: 'I live the perfect life. With several women in my phone memory'?"

"No," she says, stands up, presses a kiss on my cheek, and disappears. And who can't sleep again? Me! I should post this.

~~~

I could get up or just lie down, do the math, and feel confirmed that I'm a whiny, relationship-dysfunctional man. But do I feel uncomfortable or comfortable with the thought? On the other hand, I could also run a lap—do something for the sake of health and run the Weltschmerz from my heart again. Besides, my cheeseburger consumption has increased at Exxtrablatt, and yet SHE no longer works there. I've no idea where SHE has gone.

I could write a letter to Sarah, once again, as I wanted to do with HER. But I could also try to put HER out of my mind.

I could redecorate my apartment. The old couch needs out anyway, since I feel the springs on the left side.

However, I could also change my style, just like we men do with every new girlfriend who finds fault with our sweaters or pants. The waistband is too high on one, too far down on the other. One likes branded clothes, while the other pays attention to fair trade. So I could go out and just buy my clothes, which I then again only have until the next relationship looks into the closet, only to hear, "Actually, your style is quite ok, but . . ."

The apartment, too, provides such a question. What's a couch for when she doesn't like it later anyway? There are no cushions, a candle must be placed on the sideboard, and why the hell don't you have any tablecloths? Discussions that creep into everyday communication. And one day, the man realizes: Damn it, I don't have an apartment anymore.

As soon as I would let a person into my life again, the person would only nag or blubber like a know-it-all. I put up with everything, because of love, only to do something wrong again and hear: "You didn't do that before" or "I used to be able to smell you, but not anymore."

But I could also get up, go to all my former

apartments with a bucket of black, paint the walls, and scream, "IS IT BETTER NOW?"

Oh, shit. I just stay in bed and go back to sleep.

~~~

After three days in bed, I have no excuses not to go to work except to ask for my dismissal because I would need a doctor to be officially sick. It's jinxed; work life forces me into the normality of a cold day. Ever experienced Linz on a foggy, rainy early summer day? Gray. Everything, even the conifers, try to match the color. My only consolation after years of travel is that it's like this everywhere I could imagine to live. When does summer finally decide to take action?

Laura writes, "And stop complaining—you always say life is great, so get up and start enjoying it."

David, in turn, writes, "She said yes!" The man also really leaves no stone unturned, and I wish him the very best.

"Find the time!" a colleague shouts at me later while I leave the office too late. The interjection was on the topic of work and leisure in this day and age. After my last attempts to find a home for my twisted thoughts, I have become a workaholic, seeking comfort in a field of activity that does not suit me at all, and yet I have developed an ambition for it. If I were at peace with myself, I would immediately abandon work and just do it satisfactorily.

At least I have more contact with my son. I see him not only at the hospital after fights but also after school, where he can be picked up. One or two streets away, of course, as he doesn't want to appear uncool. In that respect, it's fascinating how intensely that short time between being picked up, going out for ice cream or a little something to drink, and being home can be experienced. He may not care. He is my support during this time. He is important to me. *What's important to him?* Probably something else, but he's very withdrawn right now; getting through to him is complicated. It's just him being a young teenager.

Finding time. For what? Chasing a ghost? HER? Finding reconciliation with girlfriends? For me? I have time. Every night when I go to bed too early, I look at the ceiling for a while . . . This time can last more than an hour, and my mind goes blank. To numb the thoughts with television is monotonous. Computer games are predictable after the fifth level. Shit, I have mutated into a whiner. A pile of stinking self-pity. Why does nobody hit me in the face? Probably because it will hurt, and I'm a cowardly pig.

So, I'm stuck in a hole, a storm on the high seas, tied to the rock. My friends don't get it this time. This time I put up a facade. I'm at the men's vacations, the social events, joking; I am funny, I just don't want to be the center of attention. But inside, I am empty, exhausted from being me. It's got me—depression—and I don't like that at all. I'm angry with myself, and on the outside, I put up a workaholic facade. That's probably why my sister looks at me so skeptically because she doesn't know me to be that way.

So, I'm supposed to find time.

"All right," I mumble, a habit I've been consciously doing for a while now, interestingly enough. Even in a discussion, I throw in a half sentence half aloud. A bad habit, known to me, but I'm doing nothing against it. Apparently, the character continues to change. *Then I'll go to a café again.* And I find my way to the traditional Linz café Traxelmayr. The bad thing is, almost the same people are there again—the same faces—and as a café patron, it feels familiar.

So, I sit down, a newspaper in hand, and take my time in this open space with old stucco ceilings. It's hard to observe when your head is full of thoughts. I find it hard to concentrate at the beginning. Because of the late afternoon, the place is well filled, mainly with older couples and some students who provide a certain basic noise. At least no one is talking loudly on the phone with a customer, or supplier, or aunt at first.

As always, there's the quiet couple who hopefully understand each other blindly; otherwise, these two don't have much to say to each other if they don't even find it worth the effort to pick up a newspaper to kill time. Of course, the macho is there, too, making sweeping movements. The voice is in exactly the volume dosed that one understands how great he is. And I catch myself realizing how it becomes easier and easier for me to hold up the newspaper only as an alibi to watch.

It's like in a movie. Just like the long-legged creature from the fairy world that just floats in and smiles at me? No, that's too much of a movie now, but I turn around anyway, just to see who she might have meant sitting behind me. And when I turn back, seeing no one, she has taken a seat two tables away.

That's how I like to take my time, occurs to me. And my rational side throws back in discourse: *It's time to take psychological treatment. Which women do you know with adequate education?* and since I make a stupid face at this discourse with myself, or at least I think so, the fairy laughs at me.

She shakes her head with a slow movement and a smile as she turns to the waiter to order something. I just hope I didn't mutter the whole thing.

I need a break now. I lift the paper high enough and take my time reading the culture page of the *Standard*, usually a ten-second affair with me. But today, I like to linger between the lines of the article about Vienna's Rathausplatz.

When I have read every possible article, and in the opinion of having wasted enough time with it, I let the newspaper sink. I see how she, too, engrossed in a newspaper, lets her eyes wander around the room.

Dark-haired—*didn't I want to stick with light-haired?* Tall, friendly eyes, slim, almost too slim, and sitting with a straight back, the fairy appears in this room.

She is present and she knows it—a dangerous trait.

I have no idea whether the quiet couple has spoken in the meantime. The macho man is still bragging about his work, and the politician to my left is still fantasizing about tax increases. I enjoy my film. My mind imagines approaching her, falling into old patterns, and taking my time. But the politician from the nearby town hall is too distracting with his surely highly populist ramblings about possible tax increases. *Hey, asshole, you're distracting me,* I think to myself.

As the movie continues for a few more minutes, I make a decision and pay. The movie in my head has come to a cheesy Hollywood happy ending that would normally make me leave the theater in a hurry. But it is my film.

I leave the cafe and upload a Facebook status after a long time.

"Taking my time." And because it's warm enough, my steps take me a few yards further to an ice cream store where I order my classic combination of lemon and chocolate and settle down in the nearby Landhauspark. Along a promenade shaded by tall chestnut trees, the old country house in the background, I enjoy my ice cream on the bench because with too many dogs, this is probably the more hygienic place.

"Is the place on the bench here still free?" the fairy asks me.

Your mouth must be open, my brain screams into a fog of too many thoughts rising in my head. No mainframe in the world can play back as many stories and images in a matter of seconds as my brain can now. Hollywood plays a role in this.

"I'm Anna, and I found it amusing how you looked at me furtively," the fairy says as she settles down without a response. "And I have a father complex; I like astonished men," the fairy laughs in my face. And at that very moment, I say the most intelligent thing I have ever said.

"I think I'm in a movie!"

The fairy laughs, her long hair blowing in the wind, although there is none to be felt. Hollywood has arrived in Linz.

"Sorry, I'm usually more eloquent in my retorts, but it's rare that a fairy speaks to people, and now I'm uttering nonsense again. I'm just going to sit here and enjoy the moment and keep my mouth shut."

"Do that, and by the way, I was kidding about the father complex, but I like how people respond to it. When I make them uncomfortable. I get pleasure out of that."

I have no idea where she's from, but she's a)

certainly not from Linz and b) certainly not Austrian.

"I'm just visiting this city, and I thought I'd look for a congenial conversationalist who has time on his hands. And you look like you have time." She knows about her charisma and plays with it—a damn dangerous trait. A player. *Damn, she's like me.*

And she's hot. She plays. She knows her power. The woman is a genius.

Yeaaah, I have masses of time, I'll take my time, let's move to the island, do wild things, don't leave me! my brain screams in my ear. Instead I answer: "Thank you for the impression I give. Especially that I pass for an easy victim and that I like talking to a fairy. When are you going to cast a spell on me?" If I'm already talking nonsense, I can just keep doing it. The fairy, named Anna, lets out a polite laugh and licks her ice cream with pleasure.

"What brings you to Linz?"

"Don't you think this is too trivial a question?" Oh my god, now it's getting complicated too.

"Okay, pause . . . let me gather my thoughts. It never actually happens that a fairy approaches me in broad daylight."

"Getting insecure, now?" The fairy grins at me.

"No, yes, probably. What was the best thing that happened to you today?"

The fairy turns her head slightly towards the road. This woman is thinking about the words she is saying.

"First of all, this question is unexpected; I thought you were going to stutter on for a while." *Damn, where did this tall, leggy beauty come from?*

"The best part of my day was spending the day today in this city, testing if it lives up to its reputation of being a prudish but beautiful city."

"And what's your conclusion so far?"

"Architecturally, this city is not the absolute hit, especially with new buildings, but otherwise it has its hotspots, with backyards, an old town, the Danube Park," smiles the fairy, whose dialect I can't place at all.

"Can I hire you for tourism promotion in Linz?"

"No, we fairies only do magic and don't bother with normal people."

"In that case—thank you for making an exception for me."

"Anyone can make a mistake," she laughs at me. "Maybe I just need a project to keep me from getting bored."

At this moment, SHE is walking along the promenade in a hasty step. Linz is just too small. My eyes wander along with her step.

"Oh, so you like that type over there— interesting." Anna pulls me out of my daydream.

"It's a short story that I'll tell you on the fur in front of the fireplace with a bottle of red wine," I say tiredly. Anna is silent and has another sparkle in her eyes. She seems sensitive. She has recognized my mood swing. *Shit*.

"Here's my e-mail address. Convince me to answer you. I don't know what, just tell me about an event here in this city. A great experience of your life. Captivate me with your lines." She hands me a piece of paper.

"I'll have to find the right words."

"Then find them," the fairy speaks and rises from the bench. She stands in the sun for me for a moment, waves, and floats away towards the city center. *What legs, what a figure!* Hollywood has left Landhauspark.

I spilled on my pants. I guess I was so fascinated by the conversation that I didn't notice the ice cream melting under my hands. "Shit," I mutter, and I don't mean the ice cream. "How can that be? Five minutes and it's all over," I catch myself muttering again.

A woman with a dog sitting next to me smiles. She probably just listened to how I made a great impression. She strokes her dog and smiles at me. Women with dogs, I swore, are no longer for me. Such a dog would certainly be a good means for a pickup. But such a big golden retriever? She seems nice, attractive, doesn't have her natural hair color but has alert green eyes, blonde. *What am I doing?*

I remain seated for minutes, letting the ice soak into my pants, contemplating the dog lying there comfortably, and letting the experience sink in. Time will sort it all out. I get up, still slightly dazed, and steer my legs home. I need a familiar, closed environment now and nod to the dog. He doesn't nod, but his mistress nods back imperceptibly. *Should I?*

I am confused. Why me? Why me, of all people? Can Hollywood be true?

Overcoming a slight feeling of hunger, I settle down at a bakery near the park pool, where one can sit comfortably outside. With a concise menu in hand, I order myself a snack. The restaurant is occupied to the extent that there is no other table free. There are only married couples, persons in a relationship, and now me. After ordering, I take a piece of paper out of my pocket. I hold it in my hands and think about the deeper meaning of her last words. *What a beautiful summer day I have had today!*

I have a door now, and I know I can't just send

an e-mail saying "Hi." It must be something that captivates this woman for a short time, lets her read the first three lines, and doesn't make her delete me right after. But what does Linz offer in the way of extraordinary events that she doesn't know about? The woman I don't know. That I don't know anything about except that she's on my mind right now. And I would like to write her an e-mail right away. Is she on Facebook?

I wrote an e-mail. Well . . . I wrote about fifteen, but only one was considered worthy of the *Send* button. And there was nothing about extraordinary events that would take place in Linz. Furthermore, I managed to wait three days. I considered it not too pushy but also not too "I don't care about you." I wrote something and sent it with the idea of a "slap" at the end, after which she smoothly wrote back that she wants me to elaborate on this topic. Thereupon my brain, deeper regions, stomach, heart, and cerebral cortex cheered exactly in that order. The "slap" did it. *I am good! I know what women want. I still got it.*

She answered, and I wrote dozens of e-mails with her back and forth. I got too excited about these e-mails again. Now I'm sitting here at the Steffel at St. Stephen's Cathedral in Vienna, in the middle of all the tourists and busy Viennese, or elective Viennese, who hurry across the square to stroll, look, talk, cry, laugh; there is a lot to see on this square. I'm too early—I'm always too early. I can't take it anymore and think to myself in the warm sun that cooling down would be good and go to the cathedral. No sooner than I am in the cathedral, a WhatsApp message is displayed: "you have your glasses on today ;-)" So, she also sits in the square too early. A laudable attitude; Hollywood is just a real dream factory.

I hurry back and see her sitting in the middle of a group of Japanese tourists. The woman, who is above average tall, stands out of the small crowd and laughs. I laugh. Again, an image that will eat into my mind, and I will never forget.

"Hi, Anna."

"Hi. Didn't you want to show me something new in Linz?"

"No, Fräulein from northern Germany who is visiting Vienna. Here, it's also nice."

"Then I look forward to a day with you where you can show me something new here," speaks the fairy and rises among the mortals and glides beside me, chattering through the alleys of the city center and in cafés, then lies with me in the meadows of the park. I feel happy right now. Reminiscent of the day back with HER lying on the Donaulände in Linz. Only my sarcasm in the conversations lets her brood occasionally. Therefore, her hands play nervously with every piece of paper as soon as we sit in a café. An interesting afternoon passes with her in the increasingly warm city.

When hunger and thirst drive us to a nearby pub, we pause at the entrance. At once, a fleeting touch, electricity running through my body—the brief kiss and the fairy glides in front of me into the pub, leaving me to trot along happily confused.

This is how my day should always end.

We sit by the window overlooking a small backyard, slightly worn but radiating a certain charm, my hand resting in hers.

"Where did you get that weird scar on your upper arm, by the way?"

"Are we lying on a fur in front of the fireplace with a glass of wine in hand?" I ask back cheekily.

Anna grins and reaches for the menu.

"I think I'm dysfunctional in relationships," she says as she reads through the menu, "and so are you." Silence.

I process syllable by syllable. My brain tries to reconcile the day with the words, recalling the e-mails; nothing has pointed to it.

Sheer horror spreads through me. Images of the last year come up. I see billboards, unrestrained drinking, and the saying "Take your time" running through my brain in a split second.

"What are you ordering?" the fairy, who has just become unapproachable, asks me.

"Uh. I'm digesting the previous sentence so that I won't be consuming anything substantial." Hollywood just became a nightmare. Horror movies play in my head, axes murdering people. Austrian cinema movies that always end tragically come to mind. Life is cinema. But always without a happy end.

The fairy tilts her head, gives me her kindest smile, and continues to study the menu.

Shit, why me! I think to myself. *I need Sarah or Laura right away—they have to translate what's going on here!* screams in my head, which is currently afraid of the impending intoxication.

I smile back. A forced smile. "Great, me too. That makes us the majority at the table." The fairy from another universe smiles at me and has suddenly slipped out of reach into fairyland.

"And why?"

"Because it's complicated, and now is not the ideal time to explain."

"Is there an ideal time?" All I get in reply is a look that makes the fairy seem human.

"A classic Schnitzel when I'm already in

Vienna, because they are simply huge here," I try to change the subject.

"You don't need to unpack your sarcasm now, just to appear confident!" comes back as an answer.

"That wasn't sarcasm; that was my response to your question earlier." There's a break there in the communication. A wall. Huge. Impenetrable. Threatening.

"But you are being sarcastic. You're trying to use it to appease your grudge, to appear cool. Just be you. I like you that way."

The rest of the meal is bumpy. I can't find the right words anymore. Her hands stop playing with napkins. As we leave the restaurant, my hand seeks hers, and she squeezes it tightly as we wander through Vienna.

"I'm going to the hotel now," is the signal to end the date after an hour, and we walk to the subway.

"Do you still want me to take you to the hotel?"

"No, it's better this way." She turns to the vending machine, and at this moment, I take the only photo I will have of her, blurred, turning to the vending machine in hurried steps.

Then suddenly, a long kiss follows, and the fairy, who was briefly in the land of the normal, takes a seat in the mundane subway. She looks at me with shining eyes, and the doors are closed.

Great date. From Hollywood to hell in five hours. That would be a typical Austrian short film. Except that the main character also gets run over by the subway.

A WhatsApp comes in: "If I had been alone, I would have done my favorite thing in such situations. Banging my head on the edge of the table

. . . Thank you . . . Sorry . . . I'm a disaster."

Me: "It's ok with fairies, they're allowed to do that . . . you were probably not feeling too well or it was not mundane enough . . . I try to understand (which is a lie) . . . stay as you are !!! And sorry for confusing you."

Fairy: "I'm not."

Me: "Then you know why anyway :) It doesn't matter why it is, and pondering doesn't help."

Fairy: "I don't."

Me: "You're a disaster :)"

Fairy: "Yes, and you cover your insecurity with sarcasm."

Me: "Then we are both a disaster. Will we meet again?"

Fairy: "I don't want to get broken by you."

Me: "Will we meet again?"

Fairy: "No"

The End. Now that would be a Facebook status. But why is she so full of sarcasm? The platform is empty. *Shitty idea to have taken your time.* Instead, a text from Amy, suddenly: "Are you actually in a relationship again?" *Oh, man, what's wrong with me?* I will change my mobile number.

~~~

Michael and David are sipping their coffee. They've been at it for five minutes. Silently. Thoughtfully. Mulling over their choice of words.

"You're a douche." Great thought.

"No, you're a chump." Very sensitive.

"Thank you."

Sip. Silence.

If anyone was watching us in the Cubus café, they would notice a group of three men only occasionally dropping a word and think to themselves, what are these characters doing? It must have been a funeral.

"Of course you are!"

"Stuffed full of self-pity and sarcasm."

"Thank you."

Sipping the third coffee.

"But you didn't deserve it either."

"No wonder, with his behavior."

"Thank you."

I think of beer, wine, tequila, vodka. And of a hole in the ground to hide in.

"Shall I summarize your last years?"

"I don't have that much time. I have to get back to the office later!"

A hand rests on my shoulder.

"First of all, why do you always find the complicated or fake witches, and why the hell do you screw up when you find one of the few right ones? Then why don't you keep working on the relationship once it is solid or recognize signs that you should end it right away?"

"Thanks," I grin weakly by now. "AAAHH!" comes out of my mouth too loudly. *Shout it out.* Yes, now I've done it—everyone here in the pub has noticed us with this.

"I quit yesterday."

"That too? Just like that?"

"Yeah, it just didn't work out. In the job, you know, I was just unhappy. What I will do in six weeks, I don't know yet. But anyway, it's better than letting myself get dragged down there too."

"Please not soooo loud," Gina, the waitress, whispers in my ear. I wince, David grins, and Michael still looks at me in disbelief.

"Well, when you go for something, you really go

for it, don't you?"

"Yes, otherwise maybe nothing will change, and on my son's birthday I'll try to sit down in my ex's garden and celebrate his birthday with him so that I can have him for once."

"I'm just afraid that you are serious about this and envision police operations and dog squads."

I grin weakly. "I'd love to, but then what good would it do me to be locked up for trespassing? Then I'd lose all contact. I just feel like doing something crazy."

"Get married."

"You're crazy. I've failed twice."

"But it would be crazy!"

"You're right, and which of the last ones should I convince? Better none; they're quite happy without me. Besides, I'm just thinking of your baseball bat story."

"Just be you again. And stop brain-wanking," David adds, though I'm already not taking the subject seriously.

"Does she still write to you?"

"Which woman?" I try to be funny, but it's just superimposed sarcasm. "Anna writes to me occasionally; Sarah too. Amy does once a month, and also otherwise, there are occasional messages from women who are neither my sister nor my mother. And they all remain—thankfully— meaninglessly superficial."

"You are lucky; I hardly ever get a text from my girlfriend."

"It's probably because of your lack of empathy when someone is down," I say and immediately regret it. "I'm sorry, I know you care about me."

A nudge to my leg from the side makes me turn around. A golden retriever drops heavily beside me—actually, on top of me.

"Sorry, I'll put him somewhere else right now," a female voice says from behind me.

"Don't worry, he can stay lying there. He doesn't look like he's homicidal and interested in my leg for food." I turn around with a grin. The face that smiles at me is familiar, as if I had seen it for months.

"Thanks, but I'll tell you right away he doesn't speak Russian!"

"Uh, what do you mean, Russian?"

"Just saying, the experience of a lifetime. Thanks for letting him lie there," she says, sitting down with her back to me.

"You're even screwing up the dog pickup thing," David whispers to me, and Michael has to control himself not to have a laughing fit.

"Yeah . . . well, it doesn't matter."

"Do you know Watzlawick? The psychotherapist? You know, I'm thinking of a story he told. And it can be applied to your love life. There was a man who lost his keys in a big pile of snow at night."

"You're kidding me now."

"Wait and hear me out! So, he lost his keys and went looking for them a good distance away," he says, pointing out of the pub.

"After a while, a man comes to his rescue, and they both keep looking. Later, the helping man asks where exactly he lost his keys, and the man points to the pile of snow." He makes a sweeping motion and points to our beers. "The helping man says, 'Then why the hell are we looking here?'" and David points out into the street again. "'Because I have light here, through the street lamp.' That's how you choose your relationships. That's how you love, yet you're the nicest person I know."

Michael laughs himself to death. Gina scowls, and I am just flabbergasted. The dog leaves, and I have the feeling that the woman behind me is also laughing.

I do not manage to get off the fence for the rest of the evening. By the end of the day, I'm too tired to post anything. A text from Sarah: "How was your day?" It doesn't get more banal than that.

A text from Laura: "I hope you find yourself." That's nice.

~~~

More often, when you just don't expect anything, then it happens. I guess because you are not prepared for it, you don't expect it and so you are more open. Anyway, it happened. I have to brush up on my English skills, but it suits my Chinese rice farmer vision. Yes, I found her, although she comes from Europe.

"You are my crush. You had me at hello!" is my favorite phrase, which Claudia then texted me days later. I sat in the café—where else—but in this case, abroad. She entered it, and at some point, we started talking in the confinement of the café, although she did not appear as a fairy. But there was a spark. No—it hit. Let's forget about HER, Sarah, and all the other women I just ran into. All other women become nothing, a speck of dust in space somewhere. Because I can only think of her. She can become HER.

"If I had the possibility to generate a time bubble, I would dwell in it with you and do everything that needs to be done." Lyrics like that blow even a self-absorbed guy like me away. Or was it just a few drops of water falling on parched earth?

I don't know. I don't give a shit, either; I'm happy, infused with feelings that even surpass HER.

"You don't touch . . . you in some weird natural but still dominant way 'grab.'" Even Michael needed an English dictionary for this when he and David asked a little more precisely at the joint couples' dinner for five—what irony. The girls were delighted about such words, even if they did not come from my mouth but from the mouth of a woman. A woman who knows exactly what to say. A marketing professional. *Damn it, another phony— maybe that should warn me?*

"What does she look like?"

"Tall, short hair, dark eyes, an interesting face, insane charisma, exactly not my type, actually," I try to grin.

"Yes, I notice that she does NOT captivate you; you write messages all the time. Where is she actually from?"

"She is definitely not Asian with rice-farming tendencies, but European, I would say, because she travels everywhere and lives everywhere and yet is not at home. We talk in the universal language, and I have enormous catching up to do there. Besides, we try not to have a relationship. Why should we? She travels, she's always somewhere, and it only goes to shit anyway, so no too-deep feelings. At least, that's what we've decided for now." I can feel the pitying looks, the thoughts of *Now he's making it too complicated for himself again, that's surely going to shit.* "And as it's going right now, I'm satisfied." Pause. "Ask me again in eight weeks," I grin weakly as my smartphone vibrates in my pants.

I can tell David wants to tell the Watzlawick story or the one about how I got a blue face.

The girls look at me. "What does she write?"

"I don't know. I'd have to look it up now," I try to play dumb. I squint at it, "but you have had it. already. at least my internal world. you turned it to a bit of chaos." I look at them and lie to their faces. "Nothing special, just what I'm doing right now."

"You're smiling," I hear.

"Yes, I also no longer have to quote the favorite saying from the show *House*: 'I am fine, but I am not happy.' She makes me beam, she makes me dream. But everyone can do that at the beginning of getting to know each other, as I've noticed with myself."

"And what's her catch?"

"I don't know her yet, but looking back at my other relationships, I'm sure there's something huge to come." I smile at the group.

If they knew what mystery was to follow, I think to myself, feeling my insides rise up against this woman as it consumes itself on the other hand. Chaos—yes, it will be. "That I will try to rationalize this all to myself. And therefore maybe feel like we shouldn't," comes as a following text from her. *Shitty chemical feeling*, I think to myself while my soup bowl crashes to the floor with a loud noise. Fortunately, this changes the subject.

"I am not sure why exactly I do like you. But I do," is the last message in the evening that lets me fall asleep smiling, although I should be pondering over it.

~~~

I have become a traveler. Actually, a frequent flyer. One week in London, next month in Prague, then maybe Oslo. I visit Claudia where she is working, but never where she lives. She does the same. We have no idea how the other one lives. David wanted to know if that would help. I don't really have a good answer for that. I miss her when I don't see her, so I'm glad when I see her. Maybe it is also good not to have a normal life with her. In normal life, boredom creeps in. And I have never been able to cope with that.

Besides, I love our text communication that gets even me involved in the emotional turmoil, because her words, for whatever reason, touch me deeply. And most of all, I love her energy. When she touches you, it feels like you're standing still in time and drawing strength from the universe. How do I come up with such bullshit? I don't know, and I don't give a shit now.

Today, I'm in Madrid. Beautiful city. I even have time to visit it because of the two of us, she is the one who has to sit with the customer. I can retire to a café with my work and taste the Spanish cuisine. Gradually, I'm getting fat! This traveling completely messes up my eating rhythm. I can't make up for this constant lunch with irregular exercise.

"There isn't room for anything that common, as we are absorbed by the energy we usually only send out . . . not receive." Such sentences blow me away. She sits there in her meetings and writes these things on the side. The woman is busier with her brain than I am—my female clone.

"Do I already have to polish the baseball bat?" Michael asks.

If he knew what a surprise there would be. I have to grin, subdued, because it is, in fact, not so funny.

She appears. She doesn't enter the door of the restaurant. She just appears, filling the room with life and feelings as men and women turn to look at her. But her eyes belong only to me. They focus on me, shining, and while she is coming towards me, people move away from her. And then she sits down opposite me. The first incredulous looks of "*That one?*", that I get from other guests, are already known to me and amuse me again and again, but they also make me aware of what she probably sees in me. I am with her. She is there. I am happy.

"How was your day?" the most trivial of all questions is always our introduction should we not see each other until later. And it is exactly this question that makes the difference because it is heard, answered, and grasped.

"I was distracted by you, I had a successful conversation and can announce with joy that I don't have work tomorrow. Do you have time then?" she asks me. Me, the guy who sees work only as purpose, not fulfillment. Of course I have time; for sure, I have time.

Her hand rests on my thigh. She plays with me, increases the pressure. Looks at me innocently and yet is so full of passion. I know that she plays; let it happen, because the moment is simply brilliant, unforgettable. I see the images that burn themselves into my brain, and I know about the end. I touch her. I see the excitement in her eyes; she doesn't care where she is. She takes my energy and gives it back. Sheer, pure feeling.

Paying—separate bills. She insists on it. A violation, once tried, is punished with sex withdrawal, and I definitely don't want to be deprived of sex. Besides, why should I argue with her? Not with this sex, where two alphas live it up in bed.

And just like that, she grasps my arm. And I grasp her, too; her mouth is open, moaning slightly in the middle of the restaurant. Is this love or pure sex? After four months now? Do I already miss her when I don't have her around me? Yes, I am immediately sleepless again. On the other hand, I occasionally miss Sarah's mischievous comments, the soft look of HER, Anna's beauty, and what they were all named and called. But Claudia has dived into all the areas that are important to me: she perceives me, lives with me. Once she said to me: "I had a feeling, I adore your experience, your wisdom. Whatever it is, you know that it is what makes me . . . relaxed. comfortable."

The early evening ends late at night. Snuggled close together, we can't let go of each other. These nights are sleepless but immensely more intense than when I would lie alone in bed.

A no-brainer.

We talk, knowing we can't sleep because the desire is just too strong every time. We use the time together well because we are not allowed to be in a relationship. We can't. "You and I can't be a couple," or as she once wrote: "You have been married/have no religion/have a lot of scars/my first baby wouldn't be yours/different age/and you try to think too much, but all these things make me love you at the same time. So cannot have a relationship." A no-brainer.

"We have to draw up a contract so that we don't slip into a relationship—with penalties, because we tend to do that, and me and you don't want a relationship." *Do I really not want that?* my brain screams. Yes, I do, but I don't dare say it; maybe it's too early. Besides, there's something else that my friends can't know, because otherwise they would really punish me.

And in the middle of the night at three o'clock

in the morning, she lies with her head on my belly and produces a document.

No.	Rule	Punishment
1	We will never have a relationship	We will get married at once on the very day
2	We will never fall in love	Got to cook for the other for an entire year
3	We stay in touch whatever happens	Got to pay a €500 fine to the other
4	No presents	Got to get their parents and siblings gifts as well
5	Being honest about other friends with benefits	Has to introduce them
6	No parties together	Has to pay for everything
7	No dates with friends	Has to donate €20 to a charitable organization
8	Never call each other	Got to give the other massages for one week
9	No wellness trips	Got to pick up a sport that the other chooses
10	She picks the music	She also picks the TV program
11	No cooking together	Got to be there for the other one three days and nights in a row

There is laughter while we sign. We do not take it seriously, or at least I don't think so. I love her with all my heart, and around five, also physically. Damn, I have violated at least two rules now alone.

When she falls asleep, I take a picture of her

sleeping face because I know that any time could be the last time.

~~~

"You're not together anymore?"

"We never were. Did you forget the contract?"

"Contract? Hey, you're crazy! You did that on a whim! On a high of feelings and because you're both insane, and because you'll never be able to do anything normal anyway." Michael is simply beside himself.

"When did it end?"

"Friday, two weeks ago, after I drove her to London from Rome."

"You were where and did what?"

"I went through Austria-Rome-London-Austria in one week." I follow up with a sad look.

"And you haven't told me since? What the hell made you go to Italy and fetch her?"

"I was going to—well—tell you, but I wanted to wait and see how their honeymoon went."

Michael is stunned, as so often when it comes to me and the subject of women.

"What honeymoon? Hey, boy, you're killing me—are you married now? What's wrong with you?!"

"Probably just had an affair with a taken woman and hoped there would be a happy ending for him," I hear a female voice say behind me. "Sorry to jump in on this, but your love life has been with me for months now here in this town." I look at the woman, not knowing her, but yet her face seems familiar until I spot the dog at her side—the golden retriever.

"Yes, unfortunately, I was privileged to see

you often with different women. Additionally, you use the same pubs as I do, so by now, I know too much about you because he," she points to Michael, "can't talk in a low voice."

"What the fuck does it matter now? Affair? Wedding? Trip? Who is married? You? You knew it all along and yet you raved about her so much? What's going wrong with you?" Quite a lot at once for the best friend who would get you out of hell if he only knew which one.

"Yes, hence the contract to make us aware not to fall in love or start a relationship. Didn't work out, of course. That's why we saw each other even Friday."

"Fuck the contract." It escapes him.

"You're cuckoo," the stranger says.

"Real mad!" says my friend next to me.

"Now, before we go on throwing niceties at each other, may I introduce myself?"

"No," replies the stranger firmly. "First of all, I know your name. I even know where you live, and don't ask me why; you know too many people here in Linz. And secondly, I don't want to be on your hit list because that is supposed to hurt, I've been told. You are nice and also certainly my type, but you produce too many corpses on your way."

"Her first name is certainly Sarah," Michael squeals, still looking at me without comprehension and earning a skeptical look from her.

"Okay then, no name, that's Michael," I nod in his direction, and she looks at him as if they had been enemies for years.

"Back to you, douchebag," Michael snaps at me. "So you knew from the start that she was engaged." I nod. "That this had no future, yet you met up all over Europe when one of you was away, and then you picked her up from Rome and took her to London and then waited there until she got married? My good old friend, you watch too much TV, and you're mad. That can't have a happy ending."

Secretly, I'm glad that David isn't here, but I'm sure he'll give me a telling-off. He'd better plan his wedding.

You're right with your assumption, I think to myself. *I was hoping that she would realize her feelings towards me on the road trip and skip the wedding.* The blonde is getting closer. Though I knew exactly what she felt for me, maybe still feels.

"I hoped to inspire her with this move, but she has always said in passing: 'You are in my inside world, I can feel you, but I am not willing to move it anywhere further. I have a bond I can't describe with my fiancée, but I love you'—so it was tricky from the start."

"What a story," the blonde interjects, the dog still napping.

"On the other hand, it was cool to do this road trip. I saw and experienced a lot in those few days."

"He's really crazy!"

"Yeah, he's like that. He always goes full risk, hitting the concrete wall at two hundred. Running blindly through the world and hoping for the best. It's clear that this was doomed to fail. Did you at least have sex during that time?"

What a question. "Yes, once. Otherwise, we slept from all the driving."

"God, you always manage to amaze me. I'd just like to know why?"

"Why? Because I love, because I'm excited, because I'm jumping in at the deep end, because I see an opportunity, because it inspires me."

"Almost every one inspires him," comes an

unnecessary comment.

"I feel comfortable with her—and don't say now that I do with everyone—and I just had timeless moments. Because a kind of energy was flowing there that I've never felt before. Because she was at my core, because she was just there. Oh, shit!"

"So why does it never work?" asks Michael.

"Because people don't dare jump into the deep end anymore. They have their job, which they often don't love, their habits, the traditions—because something always spoke against jumping. Nobody dares anymore. I do. I go to lakes, I get beaten up, and I drive through the world, experiencing the other one. In her case, because it was an 'obligation,' because she gave him her word to marry him, and because she has known him for years. She has known everything. I'm just new, and you don't know how it ends. I am the cold, unknown deep water. I am the evil foamy sea with all my experiences, the scars, the background noises, and then nobody dares anymore but prefers the warm, old-fashioned mantelpiece. In itself, it's not a stupid idea."

Sarah didn't want to; Anna, SHE, Amy, all of them find explanations why it can't go on, but none dares to get over it. But then they still write regularly, don't want to break off contact, and the idiot, that I am, still hopes with everyone that there might be something again.

"But above all, they can't deal with my past, my ever-growing number of women. Look at her," pointing to the stranger. "She knows me by now because I have a corpse in her group of friends. Great prospects." I take a sip from the beer glass. "Funnily enough, it is not likely to be my character. It was even once my bodily odor, which was disturbing—that made one leave me." The blonde nods as if she were an expert in it.

Green eyes. Just cool, green eyes.

"Besides, we men are now the better women and can't cope with the current image of women. Do you even need us anymore?" Michael wants to respond; the stranger grins as if she had won the lottery.

"But in the end, we fail to listen, to respond to the other person, to find the time, and to dare to jump into the deep end. It is a pity." I direct my gaze at the stranger. "Are you sure you don't want to join me for a coffee? I know a very cozy bakery."

"I think you know a lot of places for a lot of occasions. It has to be a place where you've never been with a woman."

"That will be difficult with him," Michael must interject.

"And even if you were the last guy on this planet, I certainly wouldn't go for a coffee with you."

The dog lifts his head and seems to nod to this.

"Thanks for the drastic rejection. Then why are you actually talking here?"

"You're funny."

Now Michael is grinning like a Cheshire cat. I need something to drink, even if it's just a glass of water.

"Why did you go all over Europe with her, anyway?"

"Because I tried. Because I tried everything to maintain that feeling. But she chose to experience, what she already knew, and a promise over cold water."

"Understandable," the woman next to me interjects.

"But then why did she do it, anyway?" I look at her.

"I can't tell you that. I wouldn't do it."

"See, in the end, women are more complex than that. You don't even understand yourselves. With me, at least you could break it down to the point that I wanted to fuck her."

"Idiot," comes out of Michael's mouth for a change. "Sometimes you just talk shit because that certainly wasn't your primary motivation."

The blonde rises. "Gentlemen, it has been a pleasure to be a part of this conversation for a brief moment, and I would like to give you some advice. First, get yourself checked out before you get anywhere near a female because there are certainly diseases on you by now that no human has seen yet. Second, don't think so much, and third, maybe you should just open up to a different type of woman."

"To you?"

"Not even when the hell freezes over," she says and leaves us. You never hear clearer statements than that.

Michael glares at me. "If you post anything now, I'll sink your cell phone in the Danube."

"No, I'm just sad."

"I also don't know why it just doesn't work for you. You probably really have a knack for complicated relationships. I'm sorry. But please do me a favor. LEAVE IT ALONE. I don't care if you get a new mobile number, change your name, change your address, and stop calling all your old numbers. Give it a rest. Sit back. Work. We care about you— just please don't put your heart through that pain again. Because we care about you, so please don't break yourself."

Pleading.

Honest.

To the point.

A friend. *The* friend. A rock.
"This is how we'll do it."
"And stop posting on Facebook!"
"That's not how I do it!"

~~~

My son is with me. A guys' weekend is slowly coming to an end. He has grown up. His thoughts seem focused. He continues to be my rock, and unfortunately, he is also winning more and more often at card games.

While cooking, we tried a new recipe that we definitely didn't like, and we both opted to order a pizza from the nearby restaurant. It won't be long now, and I can go for a beer with him, provided he wants to be seen together in town with his old dad. And soon, he will probably lose his heart himself. I'm a little scared for him. What if I can't be there? I'm not often there anyway because he's not in my direct vicinity.

I like these rare moments with him. They let me fall asleep blissfully in the evening. Once a week. Otherwise, I am just restless. "I am fine, but I am not happy," I, unfortunately, remember often when I still lie awake and think over the last two years.

"Why don't you date women anymore?" the teenager asks. I think about it for a moment. The last more intimate experience with a woman was more than nine months ago now. I even paid my 500 euro fine resulting from the contract with Claudia, even though it was against Michael's rule. And one week later, I got only a photo with the content that the money was forwarded to a charitable institution. Without comment. Without an inspired text. Only a photo. The woman is harder on herself than I am on myself.

"Because I'm kind of a burnt child. I mean, it just doesn't fit. I will find my Jill," I reply and have to explain to the teenager what Jack and Jill are all about. He only understood when I said that my Jack just didn't fit to his mother's Jill. And because I'm there, I tell him about the last few years, leaving out one thing or another, but trying to explain to him why it's the way it is now.

Ben is watching me. He asks a question or two. Right now, he is a young adult, no longer a child. It is a conversation between friends. I try to see it the way it is. Talk about my mistakes. The wrong expectations that people change, and above all that, everybody is different, and every relationship is different. And about precisely that, I can talk a lot.

It feels good that Ben is listening. The bell rings.

My son jumps up and runs to the door while I try to make the pizza boxes disappear. "Who is it?" I call after him. But for a while, nothing comes back.

When I try to follow him into the hall, he calls out, "Stop! Stay outside." His voice seems rushed, tense. I hear a female voice.

My ex-wife better not show up in my apartment, I think to myself and sit down on the couch.

After five endless minutes, the door opens.

He is standing in the room. In the background, I hear that someone else is in the apartment and is probably taking off their shoes.

He looks at me. He grins slightly.

"Dad, I think your life really doesn't run on a linear basis. Aunt Mary sometimes says that you are a bon vivant, a diehard optimist, and that you always see only the good in people, and above all, you are a dreamer. But I thank you for telling me all this today, and I am glad that you are my father."

I'm starting to get scared about who's in the room behind him taking off their jacket.

"I don't know the woman who's about to walk in here. But I'm going to dash home on my bike now and leave you guys alone. She's nice, though. I think she's ok, and she's up to something with you, I think. Just stay yourself." My son grins at me and leaves without saying bye-bye. The guy just turns around and leaves.

"What the hell is going on right now?" I call after him, trying to get up.

The kid turns around and leaves, just like that.

I see a face in the background. A familiar face. A well-known face. I see a smile.

I'm astonished at first—then I have to grin and know everything is okay now, or it starts all over again. But right now, two people jump into the cold water at the same time.

~~~

If you've enjoyed reading *Everything I'll Never Tell HER*, please consider leaving a review.

Even if your review is just a sentence or two—it makes all the difference. We personally read and appreciate every single one. Reviews help the book find its way to those who might also enjoy it. Thank you!

Please choose one depending on the country you are based in:

~ Scan Here to Leave a Review on Amazon.com

~ Scan Here to Leave a Review on Amazon.ca

~ Scan Here to Leave a Review on Amazon.co.uk

Printed in Great Britain
by Amazon

33947634R00078